Third & Grace

Jody Preister

To Dianne
God Bless !
Jody Preister

PUBLISH AMERICA

PublishAmerica
Baltimore

© 2006 by Jody Preister.
All rights reserved. No part of this book may be reproduced, stored in a retrieval system or transmitted in any form or by any means without the prior written permission of the publishers, except by a reviewer who may quote brief passages in a review to be printed in a newspaper, magazine or journal.

This is a work of fiction. Names, characters, corporations, institutions, organizations, events or locales in this novel are either the product of the author's imagination or, if real, used fictitiously. Any resemblance to actual persons (living or dead) is entirely coincidental.

First printing

At the specific preference of the author, PublishAmerica allowed this work to remain exactly as the author intended, verbatim, without editorial input.

ISBN: 1-4241-6019-7
PUBLISHED BY PUBLISHAMERICA, LLLP
www.publishamerica.com
Baltimore

Printed in the United States of America

To Melissa...dreams really do come true.

Contents

Chapter 1
Suddenly Single

"Get the gun! Get the gun!" she screamed at her son as the loaded pistol went flying out the door.

What thoughts must have been racing through his mind as he forced open the door and found his mother and her long time companion fighting on the floor like two mad dogs! Still, somehow, he managed to break his attention away from the obscene sight in front of him and snatch up the weapon, then turn, and propel it across the road and into the lake.

That was January 7, 2003; a day that would change the life of Judy Braxtin forever.

It wasn't as if changing her life hadn't happened before. After all, she had left her husband of many years for this idiot, which she now refers to as "Dr. Dickhead", nearly ten years prior to this cold January evening. Now, dazed, confused and bruised from the beating she just received she sat in a cold pickup, shivering, as her belongings were tossed into the back ends of various other pickup trucks, which her son managed to gather together in a moment's notice. As she stared into the darkness ahead she thought to herself, "Ten years…ten years of my life I gave to this man…ten years!" Wearily her mind went back to that fall day when her life made a previous dramatic change.

It was a windy evening. There was a romantic dinner, too much wine, and a walk along the lake in the moonlight. Then his hand reached for hers. They sat on the rocks by the lake in the moonlight and he gently leaned toward her and passionately kissed her.

How long it had been since she had been kissed like that or felt so wanted. His desire for her was powerful and she was so tired of fighting; tired of trying to inspire that same desire in her angry and hurtful husband. Her head was spinning from the wine and her heart was pounding, stronger than the waves on the lake against the rocks, from the excitement of the moment.

She knew it was wrong, but she no longer cared. She was weak, tired and just wanted someone to take her away from it all. After giving so much care to everyone else, she just wanted someone to take care of her for a change. She was empty, sad and lonely and so she caved in to him that night. He took her and he told her he loved her. Smiling through her tears she decided she must love him too. It was the only way she could justify what she had done with him. After all, she couldn't have done that with a man she didn't love.

She had crossed the line and there was no going back; knowing her husband would never forgive her and his abuse would become intolerable. It was as if she stepped outside herself; as if there had been a huge zipper down her middle and it was now undone. The old Judy slipped off onto that hotel room floor exposing a different Judy now.

It wasn't that she was happy, but she did feel a sense of relief. She felt like she was the maiden who had been locked away in the castle tower. Her new lover was her knight in shining armor sent to rescue her from the fire-breathing dragon…her husband.

Did she love this new man? Did it matter? Could she love him? She had loved a man who seemed to despise her for years, how could loving this man be so difficult? So, they each left their old lives, husband and wife, behind them and started a new life together; Dr. Dickhead and his assistant.

The truck came to a stop in the driveway of a little white house with black shutters.

"Mom, are you all right?" Brad carefully asked his mother, as he unlocked the doors so they could get out. Judy was shamefully silent. "You can stay here tonight...or as long as you need to, you know that, right?"

The truck door opened and there was a hand on her arm as Jen appeared to help her mother-in-law down from the four wheel drive pick-up. "It's going to be okay. You just rest. Don't worry about a thing tonight," she said trying to assure the frazzled figure she attempted to support.

"Oh, my arm!" Judy exclaimed as Jen accidentally pressed on a fresh bruise left there from Dr. Dickhead.

"I'm so sorry...we'll get some ice on it in the house." Jen moved her support to a less tender area and gently led Judy up the steps to the front door. There was ice on the walkway and the midnight air was so cold it froze the hair in your nose.

Judy and Jen went into the house while Brad and his friends unloaded the pick ups piled with his mother's meager possessions into his garage.

"What an ass!" Brad grunted, barely audible to his buddy, Carl, "Can you believe he had a gun?"

Carl just shook his head in disbelief as he handed down another plastic tub of Judy's junk to Brad. Then he said, "Did he always drink so much?"

"Not really," Brad responded, taking the tub from Carl, "but lately it was getting worse and worse. Ever since he started going out of the country with his work and leaving Mom behind. I guess he was screwing a hooker down there...what an ass!" he said again, this time tossing a box angrily on the pile of many.

"At least Mom was smart enough to leave him the minute she found out. I'm glad she called me tonight. I'm really glad I got there and got rid of that damn gun. But I've got to tell you, when I had it in my hands, I had to think twice about what to do with it. I'm glad now that I chose to throw it into the lake. I was so pissed and I was tempted to use it on him, but the way he and Mom were all tangled up on the floor I was afraid I'd miss and shoot her." Brad took a deep breath and leaned against the garage wall, taking a drink from his can of Mountain Dew.

"I don't know if I could have had your control," Carl said, as he stopped to light up a smoke. He inhaled deeply and released the smoke slowly between his shivering lips. "Damn it's cold tonight! Do you think she got everything of hers?" he stated, staring at the heaping pile of mayhem in front of them.

Brad turned to his friend and replied, "Nah, she had to leave some things behind because they were buried in the garage...it nearly broke her heart because some of the things were her grandma's, but I convinced her that Great-Grandma would rather have her safe and alive than worrying about some old stuff."

"Sorry about the house..." Jen said, apologetically, "I haven't felt like doing much lately." It was too early for any outward sign of the baby on Jen but Judy looked at her and just smiled knowingly.

The house was warm but disheveled and there was a strange odor in the air; a combination of full litter box smell and the scent of old garbage. There were dirty dishes on the table and piled in the sink, still holding the remains of meals from days gone by. A big orange cat was prowling over the table sniffing at the dishes to decipher if any contained something it dared to eat. On the floor, just out side of the overflowing trash can, were rolled-up used disposable diapers, which also contributed to the aroma in the house.

Brad and Jen had two of Judy's four grandchildren and they usually ran wild at their house. It would appear that nothing ever got done around there except playing. "Maybe that's not such a bad thing," Judy thought to herself, as Jen cleared a spot for her to sit on a sofa which was buried in clothes; one would wonder if they were dirty or clean.

"You can sleep in Matthew's bed...I hope that's okay," Jen offered, ignoring the chaos around her, "Matthew will just sleep with us and Jasmine is at the relatives."

Jen was a sweet girl. She and Brad had been through a lot in their brief marriage. Brad struggled daily to overcome the learned characteristics he observed of his father while growing up and Jen battled with depression. They were good kids though and, tonight, Judy was very thankful for them.

Crawling into the lower bunk bed was not only painful but challenging for Judy. Everything hurt and closing her eyes was difficult due to the amount of swelling from crying so hard. She didn't shed a single tear until they drove away from his house on the lake. Sadly, she looked for the last time at the little tan house with forest green trim and her hand painted geese above the garage door. She had worked so hard on those birds to make them look real. He wanted her to paint wildlife...so she did.

She had remained calm and appeared confident and in control against her drunken opponent. Her reflexes were quick when she found him loading that pistol with the fatal "wad-cutter" bullets he was so proud of possessing.

"These are for your son!" he slurred as he struggled to load the small hand gun and to make himself look powerful.

Instinctively, like a cat going after a mouse, her hand snatched the pistol from him and, with a very surprised look on his face; he turned to her and attempted to wrestle the loaded gun out of her hands.

Judy begged, "Stop, we can't do this! There isn't a safety on this gun! Stop!" But Dr. Dickhead didn't care and he kicked her hard in the right knee, dropping her to the floor in pain; kicking and punching and grasping for the small black pistol clutched in Judy's hands.

That was when Brad showed up. Judy had called him previously and asked him to come and get her. Brad didn't hesitate. He could tell by the tone of his mother's voice that she needed him and he responded. He was a good son.

Then, the thought of what had happened, what could have happened, hit her and the floodgates, containing her tears, released.

Although grateful for the place of safety, it was hard to force sleep. "What is that odor?" Judy wondered, glancing around the warm, pungent room barely lighted by the outside streetlights, which crept in through the Scooby-Doo sheets hanging from nails over the windows.

She wanted to crawl out and crack open one of the sheet draped windows, but she was too tired, sore and weak from the physical and emotional distress her body had been through. So she filtered the air she breathed through the corner of her grandson's comforter; thanking God for watching over her and asking him to forgive her, and then…gradually…drifted off to sleep.

Morning came and Judy was grateful for the sleep she received. She looked around the room and felt bad that she had intruded on her son's home without giving the opportunity for them to prepare for her coming. The condition of the house was not the normal situation for them and Judy knew it.

Jen was in the kitchen working on the dishes and attempting to clean up some when Judy sheepishly appeared. "Good morning," Jen said as cheerfully as she could, "did you sleep ok?"

Judy nodded, "Thanks." It was all she could manage.

"I'm so sorry about the house…are you hungry? Would you like some coffee?" Jen asked, trying to be a good hostess.

"Coffee would be great, if you have some," Judy responded slowly. The coffee was hot and strong. "This is just what I needed…thanks. I'm sorry I had to put you through this," and Judy proceeded to sip it slowly, staring blankly at the table before her. "What am I going to do now?" she thought to herself.

Jen spoke, as she set the cat down on the floor, "Brad had to go to work, but he told me to tell you that you can stay with us as long as you need to…" then she saw the tear-filled eyes of her mother-in-law and she sat down next to her reaching her hand across the table, she touched Judy's, saying softly, "It will be ok…you'll get through this…you aren't alone."

Judy smiled, "I know, I know…thanks. It's just so strange…how could I have been so stupid?"

"You're not stupid!" Jen rebuked, "He was just such an incredible liar and cheat," and they both laughed slightly.

But Judy did feel stupid. "How could I get myself into such a mess?" she thought, "I let him control everything about me…my job…my income…my transportation…my life! What was I thinking?" And she sipped her coffee.

"I'm not going back," she said with confidence to Jen, "I have to start over. I will never, EVER be someone's significant other again!" With that, she and Jen clanked their coffee mugs together as if to signify a toast to her new beginning.

The sun was shining as Judy drove her little white car down the highway headed to her daughter's home located in Harvey, a small town in Northeast Nebraska. She had called her that morning and told her what had happened the night before.

"You're kidding! You've got to be kidding!" was all Alicia could say at first. Then she scowled, "What an ass! You did the right thing, Mom. You need to get as far from him as you can. Did you call the police?"

The police? The thought had occurred to Judy, but she reflected back on the memory of conversations she overheard between Dr. Dickhead and an acquaintance. They were discussing the possibility of hiring someone to "take care of" his ex-wife, who was demanding far too much alimony, and was bitter about being dumped for a younger woman...Judy.

"If I called the police you know he would come after me...he would lose his license to practice and he'd have someone get rid of me...I know he would...I've heard him talk about it before," her voice was trembling, "I just want to get away and never see him again." .

"It's going to be okay, Mom. You're a strong woman. I'm glad you left the way you did. You don't ever have to go back. You're safe now. Did you get everything?" Alicia was doing her best to reassure her mother.

"I got what was important. They just piled stuff into pick-ups. There was no time to pack or plan. He told me I had to be out that night because he was changing the locks the next day and my stuff would be thrown out. Your brother was great. He was so strong and calm. He never lost his composure even though the Dickhead tried to intimidate him."

"What an ass!" Alicia repeated.

"Yeah, he is," Judy returned, "You know what his last words to me were? *Are you going to be at work on Monday?* Can you believe that?"

There was a grunt of disgust on the other end of the line from Alicia, "You know that's all he cared about was his money, Mom…well that and his drinking. It's amazing he functioned as well as he did with the way he was drinking."

Remembering back, Judy replied, "Well, he wasn't functioning that well anymore. I was taking the calls from the answering service in the middle of the night because I could no longer wake him from his drunken stupor. He still didn't start drinking until the five o'clock happy hour time, but then he would drink until he passed out. And he wasn't the fun drunk he used to be when we were first together. He was getting mean and abusive…I don't want to talk about it anymore…" Judy could feel the tears welling up in her eyes.

"It's ok, Mom…we don't have to. It's over now…behind you. You can move on, now, and make a new life. I'll help you. You were there for me when my marriages failed, now it's my turn to be there for you. We'll do it together. How soon will you be here?"

Judy looked at her watch, "I'm about thirty minutes away. I need to make one more call before I lose signal." So they said their goodbyes and see you laters and disconnected.

"I really don't want to make this call, but I need to," Judy said, as she pressed the voice dial on her cell phone. "Anna," she said clearly and distinctly.

The voice in her phone responded, "Did you say Anna?"

Judy replied, "Yes."

The phone at the other end of the connection was ringing and a sleepy voice answered, "H-hello?"

"Anna? This is Judy. I'm sorry, did I wake you?"

"Its okay, the baby was up a lot last night and I didn't get much sleep. I think she's teething or something. What's up?"

Judy took a deep breath to try and slow her pounding heart and collect her thoughts, "Anna, I left your father last night…"

"What? What happened?" Anna answered, much more alert now.

"Anna, I found out that he was paying for sex while on business in Mexico. He has been seeing someone down there for some time now. He was drunk...there was a gun involved...it was ugly."

"Oh my God! Are you all right...did he hurt you?" She was genuinely concerned.

"I'm ok, Anna...well...I'll be ok. He beat me up a little and the gun is in the lake. Brad came to get me and he threw it in there. I'm not going back...it's over...I wanted to call and tell you before he did so you would know what really happened."

Anna took a deep breath, "He hasn't tried to call me yet, but I'm sure he will. You said he was drunk?"

"Yes, Anna, he was...but sober enough to know exactly what he was doing. There is no excuse."

Judy could hear the uncertainty in Anna's voice when she responded, "I know...I know...but where will you go? What will you do?"

"I'm ok, Anna. I've got a little money saved, I have my car, and I'll get another job. I stayed at Brad and Jen's last night, but I'm headed to Alicia's and will probably relocate there since it provides some distance between your father and I. Alicia has a big house and there is plenty of room. I can help watch the kids for her while she works. It will be a good place for me to clear my head...you know?"

There was silence on the other end and Judy thought the call may have dropped, "Are you there?"

And a small, sad voice said, "I'm here...I just can't believe it."

Judy's eyes welled up with tears, "Anna, you know I love you. You are like my own daughter. And Mary is like my own granddaughter. That doesn't have to change if you don't want it to. I hope you know that."

Anna stammered, "I know...I hope so...I mean I want it to be that way...it's just so hard."

Both Judy and Anna knew the chance of them remaining close would be slim. Dr. Dickhead would make it very difficult for Anna. But she was a strong young woman. Judy had tried to instill those traits in her. Anna's own mother had rejected her in so many ways; often using her as a way to take revenge on her disloyal husband. Judy was the substitute mother Anna knew most of her adolescent life. They went from bedwetting to sex education to graduation together.

Anna had lived with her father and Judy on the lake and they had been through many adjustments and battles. Some battles were serious; like the time Anna decided to take revenge on Judy, for whatever reason, by putting peroxide in her contact lens solution. After a trip to the emergency room, and seeing Judy with patches on her eyes while they healed, Anna knelt by the bed and apologized through very genuine tears. It was an evil thing to do, but she had learned well how to hurt others from the example set her by her parents before.

Anna was constantly fighting for her father's attention and love. He was often cruel and hurtful to Anna; teasing her about her weight problem and forcing his control over her. He would show up at her school functions drunk; humiliating and embarrassing Anna in front of her peers. Often Judy found herself between them as they fought trying to protect Anna from one of her father's drunken rages. Anna rebelled against him and escaped through a boyfriend and a pregnancy.

"I wonder what will become of little Mary…will I still get to see her?' Judy pondered after they said their goodbyes.

She was such a sweet baby. So tiny when she was born; weighing just barely 5 pounds. How she had prayed for that sweet baby and now she was so healthy and normal…and teething. Poor Anna! Although she was strong, she was still so young and trying so hard to be grown up.

"God, help her make it and become a great teacher someday." Judy prayed inwardly, as she turned left on Highway 19…the route to her new life.

Chapter 2
Let the Healing Begin

Alicia's house was just the distraction Judy needed to get her mind off the memory of where she had been. For the first few nights Brad, Jen and kids stayed at the house, too; as if to assist Alicia in the watch over their mother. But Judy wasn't going to let this destroy her. It wasn't long before she was driving everyone crazy with her order and lists of things to do.

"Grandma! Grandma! Let's go sing some more!" Little Maggie Lu came running over to Judy and flung herself into her lap. "Let's go do laundry some more!" she would say with excitement.

Judy did all the laundry in the house. It was the one thing she felt she could do to contribute. The laundry room was in the basement, but it was a nice basement with tall ceilings and clean. She and Maggie Lu would put in the *Martina McBride's Greatest Hits* CD and sing as loudly as they could to all the songs. It was great fun for Maggie Lu and good healing for Judy as many of the songs dealt with overcoming abuse and gaining strength.

"We'll sing again when there is more laundry to do, okay?" Judy answered as she lifted Maggie Lu to her lap, "How would you like Grandma to read you a book?"

"*Pokey Little Puppy!*" Maggie Lu squealed with delight; and so they read.

Judy would help Alicia put chore charts together for the kids and assist her son, Alex with his homework. Alex had difficulty concentrating and so they made a surprise box to help motivate him to sit still and study for a few minutes at a time.

"This is too hard!" he would say, "I can't do it!"

But having the surprise box helped because if he accomplished so much time doing his homework he could pick out a prize.

Alicia cut hair at a salon in a mall in Northtown, which was quite a drive from her home in Harvey. Her wages there barely paid the rent and she counted on her child support to pay her other expenses. Sometimes that wasn't very dependable.

Judy was concerned about the financial stress created because of the amount of time Alicia was taking off work to watch over her. So she used her savings and credit cards to help out, which wasn't very smart, but Judy didn't care. She was depressed and mistakenly thought spending and shopping made her feel better.

She started accumulating things for her own house, certain that she would find a good job and be able to pay for it all later. What a good time she and Alicia would have shopping. What a mess she was creating!

"How's the job search going?" Alicia would ask each day.

"I don't know. I call or apply but nothing seems to be right. I don't want to do anything in the medical field anymore. I just want something that gives a good income, benefits and is dull and boring for a change," Judy would say, as she glanced up from the paper.

Her first interview in nine years was a total disaster. When the supervisor interviewing asked her if he could contact her previous employer, Judy burst into tears.

"Are you all right?" he asked cautiously, passing the tissue box to her across his desk. "Perhaps this isn't the place for you. Maybe you need a little more time," he said, wondering what the problem was.

"I'm sorry," Judy said, wiping the tears and catching her breath, "how unprofessional of me…I just wasn't prepared for that question and I am uncertain how to answer it for you." Then she went on in spite of herself, "Yes, you could contact my previous employer, but

I don't know what he would have to say as I left him because I lived with him for nine years and he cheated on me with a hooker!"

Needless to say that supervisor was unimpressed and suggested Judy take some time to prepare before she ever does another interview. When she got to the car she cried and cried.

At one point she thought she had a job in a meat packing plant, but then she failed the lifting test. She had hurt her back not long ago lifting chemicals for the x-ray processor in the clinic and it prevented her from doing the best she could on the test. That was disappointing as the position offered good pay, for Northeast Nebraska, really nice benefits, and it was dull and boring.

She started paying one credit card with another and only the minimum payment. It was a vicious cycle. Her savings dwindled and she cashed in the rest of her 401K. She'd have to pay taxes on it later.

One day she stopped at a nursery in Clarmar, the little town west of Harvey. She didn't know if they were hiring, but she decided she might as well try.

While sitting in the lobby a nice older gentleman, wearing blue jeans and a flannel shirt, approached her and asked, "Do you need any help?"

Judy looked up and said, "I'm wondering if you are hiring?"

He reached out his hand and said, "I'm Albert, why don't you tell me a little about yourself." It was as if he knew she was desperate and as he sat down by her he said, "What type of work are you looking for? Do you need part-time or full-time?"

Judy looked into his kind eyes and said, "I really need something full-time. I just need a job."

"What kind of work did you do before?" he asked, gently.

"I worked in a dental clinic...actually I managed several clinics...but I was also an assistant and receptionist," Judy felt her voice tremble as she answered.

"Do you know sterilization procedures?" he asked, as he got up and brought over a book placing it on the table in front of her.

"Well, yes...I often assisted in minor surgical procedures and cleaned and sterilized instruments."

19

The book in front of her was *Plants from Test Tubes, an Introduction to Micro Propagation*. She had no idea what that was about.

Then the man smiled at her and said, "Why don't you take this book home and look it over. If it is something you think you might be interested in, call and schedule an interview with Bill. He is the one you need to talk to about a job. They are looking for someone to work in the lab cloning plants. Do you know what cloning is?"

"Yes, I've heard of it...sounds interesting...thank you," and the interview was over.

Judy was so excited about the possibility of a job and something so unusual, too. She read the book every chance she got and started calling to schedule an interview with Bill at the nursery.

Every day she would call and leave a message, "Hello this is Judy Braxtin and I need to schedule an interview with Bill regarding a job." But no one would call.

Finally she contacted a secretary and stated, "Listen, I was told by Albert that I am to see Bill about a job. I have called repeatedly and left messages, but no one returns my call..."

The voice on the other end interrupted her and said, "Albert told you to call? One moment please."

The next thing she knew she had an interview scheduled for the next morning. Come to find out, Albert owned the business.

"Good luck today, Mom!" Alicia says as she headed out the door for work. "I hope you get the job...I'll say a prayer for you!"

The interview was for later that morning. Alex was at school and Maggie Lu was at pre-school.

"You can do this!" Judy told herself as she looked in the mirror.

Suddenly, as she went to go down the stairs, her foot slipped and she plunged toward the door at the bottom of the steps. Smack! Her head hit the door frame...and a large goose egg started to form.

"Great! Just what I need now!" she said, as she caught her balance and headed out the door with a bag of frozen peas in hand.

"I am such a klutz! Hopefully it won't be too noticeable." Gently, she placed the cold bag of peas against the knot on her forehead.

Bill showed her around the nursery and introduced her to several of the people working there. She was offered the job and directed to the lab.

It was a white trailer inside the greenhouse. The windows were sealed and everything was clean and white inside. There was a hooded counter with Plexiglas and a large filter system was on the back of it to purify the air inside.

"This is where the cloning takes place," Bill explained, "but Ray, the supervisor to this part of the operation, will explain all this to you."

Ray was a short, bearded man with shaggy, salt and pepper gray, hair that he hid under a ball cap. He appeared to be stuck in a seventies time warp. He seemed to constantly have a cigarette in his mouth...but not in the lab.

Ray didn't talk much. He was forty-something and never married. Apparently he was very intelligent when it came to plants, but not so smart when it came to women. They would work closely together in the lab.

"This ought to be interesting," Judy thought, as she noticed him secretly checking her out, "Just what I don't need!" She determined she would learn as quickly as she could so she could work as independently as possible without him around.

The lab provided the perfect opportunity for Judy to reflect on her life; where she's been, where she is and where she wants to go. Her days were spent in isolation and nearly total seclusion. Occasionally, Ray would stop in with instructions for her to locate a new species out in one of the greenhouses and extract some specimen for cloning. Sometimes a fellow employee would poke their head in the door curious about what was going on inside. There was one guy there who would burst open the door to try and scare Judy while she was working.

"Tom, are you trying to catch me sleeping in here?" she would say to him as he laughed and closed the door.

Judy carefully and accurately measured out the ingredients to create the agar or medium used in the cloning process. There had to be just the right amount of chemicals, nutrients and hormones for the cells to develop correctly. Everything had to be measured and weighed precisely. It was crucial for the temperature to remain stable and of course the conditions had to be sterile.

Once the medium was mixed and cooked it was poured into the sterile baby food jars or test tubes and sealed. Then the containers we were placed in pressure cookers and sterilized again. During the sterilization process Judy would work under the hood starting new clones or dividing the seedlings or small plants that had developed into medium which had been stored in the refrigerator. This process was repeated over and over.

The medium ingredients would change when the seedlings developed to a point where their root system required stimulation to grow. As the little plants matured, they would get transferred to a special greenhouse, outside of the lab with climate control conditions, until they were strong enough to segregate into the regular areas.

It was fascinating work and Judy loved it. She was creating something and it was amazing to see these new little plants; an exact image of the Mother plant. Through micro propagation the nursery was able to produce a large number of plants in a shorter time for retail. She felt her job was important, but often felt as if no one else did.

Working in the lab was a benefit because Judy didn't have to listen to the constant complaints of the workers in the greenhouses. Many of them had worked there for years and were angry about the new hires starting out with wages that were sometimes equal to or greater than theirs. Of course you're not supposed to know what others make, but it always gets out somehow. Judy was frustrated, too. Although she loved the work, the conditions were sometimes unbearable.

When she first started work it was late winter and fairly easy to control the environment inside the lab. But as spring arrived it became more difficult. If the air conditioner in the lab broke down (which it often did) the lab became an intolerable sweat-box and the little clones suffered. It was a constant battle to get anything repaired or to stimulate anyone to care. The pay was a far cry from what she was getting managing the clinics for Dr. Dickhead...but the freedom was well worth it.

Walking was one way Judy would deal with her frustrations. During breaks, and at lunch, she would walk around the park; outside and across the street. The fresh spring air was energizing for her. She loved letting the wind blow in her long brown hair and feeling her heart pound as she walked briskly around the park. She was feeling good about herself again and started considering the possibility of dating.

During down time in the lab she would work on a list of what she wanted in a man. She no longer trusted her impulses and wanted something to refer to; sort of a check off list...just in case she met someone. But she wasn't pursuing anyone. She would look and wonder, but that was as far as it would go. Ray must have sensed her need because he would try to impress her or carry on conversation.

When Judy told Alicia about him she said, "No way, Mother! He is a real strange guy...you don't need that...stick to your list!"

Judy's main contact to the outside world was a country radio station out of Northtown called KPGY or "Piggy 94.5." She listened to it all day long and felt like she knew the daytime DJs personally. Sometimes she would call the station and answer the trivia question for the day or request a song or two. Other times she called just to participate in the discussion for the morning. That station and its personalities became her friends and she was a faithful listener.

"Mom, you know you don't have to move out. We have plenty of room for you here." Alicia pleaded.

"I know you do, but you need your space...and I need mine. It's time for me to go. The house is just a few blocks away. We'll still see each other everyday, I'm sure," Judy replied.

The house was a white two story on the corner of Third and Grace Streets. The land lord, Mr. Klassen, was a sweet older man that reminded Judy of her ex-father-in-law (his good qualities) He was always working on something and genuinely concerned for Judy's welfare.

When Judy moved in, Alicia gave her a journal which she wrote on the inside cover, "To Mom with love. Here's to your new life on Third & Grace. Love, Alicia"

Judy had so much fun fixing up her new little house. It had been a long time since she fixed up a place of her own; back when she lived in Lancaster after high school, when she followed her ex-husband (then boyfriend) to his college town.

He had a full ride athletic scholarship to the University. How she envied him. She always wanted to go to college and often did his homework for him. Lenny was an excellent athlete, but not a very good student. It had always been that way ever since they met in high school. He was the jock, she was the brain. She had fallen for him hard and felt so sorry for him because he had such a bad home life, which was full of abuse, abandonment, and neglect.

He treated her terrible back then…but she loved him in spite of it all. She thought she could make his life better…change him somehow…make him happy. When she got pregnant, they were forced into marriage. Lenny dropped out of college and worked for Judy's father; then on to other jobs.

There were those moments of joy; the birth of their children and other tender moments. Lenny had an incredible sense of humor sometimes. She remembered how his eyes would twinkle when he teased. There were babies to care for and new places to adjust to because they moved twenty-two times in their years of marriage. Separating three times before their divorce, they had tried counseling, but never stayed with it for long.

The church was no real help. Abuse is an ugly thing and the church didn't want to deal with it. They were told to pray harder, read scripture, go to services and meetings and "just give it to God"…that didn't work. Judy was bitter about the church experience, but it never made her lose her faith. She knew what she believed…even though she sometimes wandered from it. But that was old history now. "A previous life," as Judy liked to think of it.

"Hey Kiddo! How have you been?" the familiar voice on Judy's cell phone asked. It was her close friend, Jessica. They had known each other since high school but she hadn't seen her since back in January and that was three months ago.

"Hi, Jess. It's good to hear your voice. I've been ok...working a lot...you know..." Judy replied.

Then Jessica proceeded with, "Well I've been thinking about you. I was wondering...um...a friend of mine is having a party...well it's a birthday party...and...well...I just didn't want to go alone...and...well...thought maybe you'd like to get out and have some fun and go with me?"

Judy was silent.

"It's just a little party. C'mon Jude! It would be good for you to get out and meet some people again!" Jessica persisted.

"I don't know, "Judy finally responded, "I'm just not sure if I'm ready for all that, just yet...it's only been a few months...I don't know..."

Jessica interrupted, "Oh c'mon...it will be fun...I'll be there...we always have fun when we're together, right?"

She was right. They did always have fun together; whether they were having a joint garage sale, as they did so often when their kids were little, or attending class reunions. It was always a good time with Jessica. It was more difficult now though. Jessica and her husband, Ted, had traveled with Judy and Dr. Dickhead on several occasions. They had established a friendship together and Ted had even invested in business with the doctor. But Jessica and Judy's friendship went beyond the relationship of the last nine years. They were friends before either of them were married, had kids and before Judy's divorce. No man could ever get in the way of that.

"Maybe it would be good to make contact again," Judy thought to herself. With a sigh she responded, "Ok, ok...I'll go with you...you say it's a birthday party?'

Jessica was quick to answer, "Uh, yeah...yeah, that's right...a birthday party for someone I know here in Shilo...but it's ok...it will be fun. You want to stay overnight here so you don't have to drive back?"

25

"Well, ok…it will be good to get away from here for a while and do something different. Hey, you need to come up and see my little house I rented sometime. It's really cute and I've had so much fun fixing it up. Since it has shag carpet and very colorful walls, I did it in a retro seventies sort of look. I even have lava lamps! Oh, and I got a dog…a miniature dachshund. Her name is Dottie."

Jessica laughed, "Sounds great…I'll do that if I can ever get away. So you'll come this weekend then?"

"Ok, I'll be there…what should I wear?" Judy asked.

"Hey, its casual…you always look good. I'll see you on Friday then…after work, right?"   "Right," and with that they said good-bye. "Well, that might be fun," Judy said to herself, as she closed her cell phone, "What do you think, Dot?" she leaned down to pat the little dachshund on the head. Dottie looked up at her lovingly and wagged her tail.

She was such a sweet companion for Judy. Alicia had found her at the humane society and just knew she was what her mother needed to keep her company. At first Judy didn't want to deal with a pet, but when she went to see Dottie, her heart melted and they bonded instantly.

"Hmmmmm, likes dogs…yes, that will have to be added to my list. Or maybe I'll just put "likes animals"…I don't want some guy who is an animal fanatic!" She laughed and prepared her meal for one, in her perky yellow kitchen, on her retro square, brightly patterned dishes.

It felt good to eat when she wanted, watch whatever she wanted on T.V. and go to bed when she wanted…alone. Well, that didn't feel so good, but at least she had little Dottie to keep her company. She loved to snuggle down under the covers by Judy's feet.

"Maybe this single life will be okay after all," she thought to herself, "Maybe I don't need a man in my life to be happy."

As Judy was finishing doing her supper dishes the phone rang and she said, "Good time for an interruption! Hello? Oh, hi Mom, how are you and Daddy doing?"

The voice on the other end of the line was soft and weak, "Oh, we're doing pretty well. We were just thinking of you and wondering how you are. How is your job going?"

Judy wiped her hands dry on the dish towel and responded, "Its okay. I get really frustrated with it sometimes because I just don't think anyone cares what is going on in the lab. The equipment is breaking down and no one ever bothers to come in and see the progress with the plants. I love what I do, but I think maybe I should consider going back to school and getting a degree in something...I don't know," Judy had received some information from the Community College in Northtown in the mail that day.

"I think that sounds like a wonderful idea, Honey. You have always wanted to go to college. This might be the perfect time for you to do so. Do you think you could get a grant or some financial aid?" her mom asked.

"I would think so...I don't know. I'll check into it sometime when I have a day off. I just thought I'd run it by you guys and see what you think. So what is new in Colorado?" Judy sat down on her black recliner.

"Not much here...doctor's appointments...you know...the same old thing. Your sister has been here to help us when she can. Sure would love to have you come visit again. Do you think you could get away sometime?"

Judy could sense the strong desire in her mother's frail little voice, "You know, Momma, I'll see what I can do. I just don't know with the new job and all, but I'll try. Maybe Alicia and the kids will want to run out for a visit. I'll see what we can put together, okay?"

"That would be wonderful. It would be so good to see you and anyone else...especially the great grandkids. The days get kinda' long around here. We just don't get out much anymore. It's just so hard and frustrating. I wish I could get to feeling better. I made a new clown outfit that I hope to wear when I get better. You should see it. It has lots of really bright colors. The kids are going to love it."

Judy's eyes filled with tears and she fought back the lump in her throat, "I bet they will, Mom. You are such a good clown. I look forward to seeing it...I'll see what I can do about getting some time off."

"That would be great, honey. We sure miss you."

"I miss you guys, too. Hey, did I tell you that I am going to a social event?" Judy said, hoping to move to a cheerier topic.

"No…oh, that's wonderful. You need to get out. Maybe you'll meet someone nice," Mom responded lovingly.

"Well, I don't know about meeting anyone, but it will be nice to get out. I'm meeting Jessica at a birthday party in Shilo. Sounds like I'm going to stay the night at their house. It should be fun. I think I'm ready for a little fun."

"I'd say so…you work so hard you need to take a break…say a long weekend in Colorado?" She was persistent.

"Ok, Mom…I'll see what I can do. I should get to bed now. Have to get up early in the morning and take care of my little plants! Tell Daddy hello and I love you both."

"We love you too, dear. Sleep well and God Bless"

Her mother always ended her phone conversation with "God Bless". It was more than just a habit to her. She really meant it. It was as if she said it in a way to signify a little prayer just for the person she was talking to. Judy loved that about her mother.

That night as she lay in her double bed with Dottie snuggled down at her feet; Judy thanked God for always being there and for his grace, though she felt she didn't deserve it. She always knew it was there and he loved her even when she made foolish choices. She realized she was healing and it felt so good.

Chapter 3
Taking Risks

Work was the same as usual. Ray asked Judy to take some samples from the various day lilies in green house number four. It would be a long day under the hood working with the scalpel, but Judy didn't mind; it was a new plant. She had been working on orchids for so long she was starting to see them in her sleep!

The DJ's on KPGY were in rare form that morning. The station stunt man, Buckwheat, was being duct taped to the wall again by some elementary school kids; usually the result of a fund raiser of some sort. He was quite a character and the various radio personalities as well as the people in Northtown and the surrounding towns were always trying to find him a new challenge to participate in. The station owner, Mark Rivers, loved to antagonize Buckwheat on the air. It was entertaining.

"Hey, Jude…you in there?" a voice called out from the front door.

"I'm in the back with the plants," Judy responded, "What do you need Susie?"

Susie worked in the green houses weeding plants, planting, and pulling orders. She had worked for the nursery for seventeen years and was one of many that complained about it but stayed anyway. In a town the size of Clarmar, you don't have many options for work unless you want to do the hour commute, one way, to Northtown, everyday.

"There's a phone call for you…some guy," Susie continued.

"A guy? Who on earth would be calling me?" Judy said, surprised, "I'll be right there."

"Hello? This is Judy…" she proceeded cautiously.

"Listen, Judy…" The horrible familiar voice began, "…I just wanted to call because someone told me you were going to break into my house…I have people watching it, you know…the stuff you left behind is just your loss…don't try it!"

Judy was stunned for a moment. It was Dr. Dickhead and she could hear a woman's voice in the background. He was obviously drunk. Looking at her watch she noted it was just past noon.

"Must have been an early day," she thought to herself. Then she took a deep breath and answered calmly, "Who is this?" Pretending she didn't recognize his voice.

"It's Roger, damn it! I'm telling you…don't you even think of trying anything while I'm gone…you hear me? I heard you were going to do that…" his voice was firm but the words slurred together and, some how, seemed less threatening. He sounded delusional.

"Listen, Roger…why would I waste my time. I don't even think of you anymore…I don't care about you…and I wouldn't do something that stupid. You are out of my life, forever. I don't EVER want to see you again or hear from you again…Do you understand that? Don't EVER call me here or anywhere else. You mean NOTHING to me!"

There was silence on the other end of the line. Then, "Fine…I just wanted to let you know…"

"Good-bye, Roger…" Clunk! Judy put the receiver down hard.

Susie was standing close by and she turned to Judy and said, "Everything ok?"

"Yeah, its fine…I'm fine," and Judy walked away with a smile. He dished it out but she had thrown it calmly back and it felt good.

The room was smoky; typical of a bar. There were quite a few people sitting around. Although Judy had never been in that place, it was a very familiar sight. She and Dr. Dickhead had spent many, many hours in places similar.

At first it was exciting for her, having never frequented places like that during her married life. Lenny, her ex-husband, did not drink which was probably a good thing. If he had, the abuse he did would probably have been worse. He would try hard to stop his abusive behavior, but it was so deeply ingrained into his soul from the example set before him by his own parents.

Even when the physical abuse stopped (after a separation and counseling) the emotional and mental abuse continued. Judy often felt the physical abuse was easier to endure; at least the bruises healed. What he did to torment her emotionally and mentally cut deep in her spirit; resulting in constant struggles with self-esteem issues.

She suddenly felt very out of place.

"Hey Jude! Over here!" Jessica's voice called out. She had a loud and happy tone.

Judy walked toward the voice and through the crowd. She felt as if everyone was staring, and they probably were, since it was a small town and she was a new face.

"Over here, girlfriend. How are you?" Jessica greeted her with a huge hug, "Hey, everyone, this is my best friend, Judy…actually we're twins…don't we look alike?" And she squeezed her arm around Judy and pulled their faces together.

Jessica and Judy did resemble each other. They were both tall with dark hair and long legs. On one of their many island trips together, Jessica had earned the nick name "Legs" because of her extraordinarily long legs. Jessica had dark brown eyes, but Judy's eyes were hazel and sometimes looked blue or green and she wore glasses most of the time. Jessica was taller than Judy and often thinner too…but both of them looked pretty darn good for being so close to the dreaded half-century mark. Judy returned a smile to all the faces peering up at them.

"Just keep smiling," she thought to herself, "You can do this…it's just a party."

As she glanced around the table, she wondered whose birthday they were celebrating anyway. Everyone seemed to be paired into couples, except for Jessica and Judy and one other guy at the end.

"Ted had to work tonight so he couldn't be here," Jessica said, in excuse for her husband's absence, "Let's sit down here," Jessica pointed to the two end chairs across from each other at the end of the table.

"Whose birthday is it, anyway?" Judy leaned toward Jessica and whispered.

"Actually there are two birthdays…my good friend, Jim, at the end of the table and his friend, Art, sitting there with his wife, Arlene."

When Judy glanced down the table she noticed Jim looking at her and he smiled.

"They are both OLD MEN this week!" Jessica said loudly so everyone in the room could hear, "They turned fifty within a few days of each other and we are here to celebrate with them."

"The half-century mark…" Judy thought to herself, "It's just around the corner…I wonder where I'll be and what I'll be doing then?" She smiled politely at the birthday boys.

Jessica leaned close to Judy and whispered, "Jim has been very anxious to meet you."

Judy jumped back, surprised, and said, "Is that what this is about? You sneak! How could you…I'm not ready…why?"

"Calm down, calm down…it's just a social event…nothing more. He's really a nice guy, my best guy-friend. I would never introduce you to someone who I didn't know with all my heart wouldn't be good for you. Just relax and be yourself…it will be okay," Jessica was doing her best to make it seem okay, but Judy could feel the tension building up inside from the top of her head to her toes.

"Have a drink, hon…it will calm your nerves," Jessica instructed, "Maybe a glass of wine?"

"Oh, all right…just one though. I want to keep my wits about me…thanks." Pulling her confidence together Judy ordered a glass of merlot. The bar didn't have anything but zinfandel, so she settled for that.

Jessica was having a good time sharing stories of the travels taken with Judy and how they occasionally smoked cigars together on the various beaches. Judy sat and smiled politely and nodded occasionally in agreement. She had quit that nasty habit when her life changed.

Jim kept looking toward her and smiling. He had a great smile, as if he could have been advertising for a new toothpaste. He was small framed, wore glasses and his hair was thinning and gray. It was his assuring smile, though, that Judy noticed the most.

As the evening progressed, Jim made his way to the seat across from Judy which had conveniently become available when Jessica excused herself to go visit with some friends in another part of the room.

"Hi, Judy, I'm Jim…Jim Sorensen…Jessica has told me a lot about you," he said, smiling that irresistible smile and reaching his hand out to Judy's as he sat down.

"Really? She has told me nothing about you," Judy said, returning the smile and gently shaking his hand.

"I know…that was a little sneaky, huh? But I wanted to meet you and she knew you would resist so she thought this might be one way we could meet. Are you terribly upset?" His voice was sensitive, strangely high-pitched, but full of genuine concern.

"No, its okay…she was right, though. But this might be just what I need. I'm happy to meet you." Judy meant it, and his smile made it easier.

They talked for some time. He was divorced and had two daughters that lived with him, was a mail carrier, and the oldest of six children. His mother and father grew up in Shilo and still lived there. He and Art had grown up together and had known each other since kindergarten. They were best friends.

Jim had a way about him that made Judy very comfortable. He was tender and showed deep emotion…for a man. He was obviously well liked by everyone in town. In spite of herself, Judy was attracted to him.

As the evening wound down, Jim reached across the table and took Judy's hand. Staring right into her eyes he said, "It was nice meeting you, Judy, and I really enjoyed talking with you." He flashed that amazing smile.

Judy returned the smile and said, "Yes, I'm glad we met and I enjoyed talking with you, too." Then he went out the door with Art and Arlene, waving as they departed.

"Well, that wasn't so bad, was it?" Jessica asked as she returned to her seat across the table.

"You sneak! You did that on purpose...leaving me there...thank you." That was all Judy had to say about it.

They went to Jessica's house where Ted was waiting; listening to music and reading the paper. "You girls want some tea?" Ted asked as he rose from the chair, "How was your evening?"

"Tea would be great, honey...it was good. Judy met a lot of people in town...including Jim Sorensen," Jessica responded, as she took Judy's jacket and hung it on the hall hook.

"And how did that go?" Ted questioned, as he looked over at Judy and grinned.

"It was fine...I mean...he's nice...I guess...oh, I don't know. He seems really nice and has a great smile...how's that!" Judy said and laughed.

They all laughed. "It's good to see you laughing again, sweetie." Ted said softly and with a knowing smile.

"How about some Scrabble?" Jessica cheerfully interrupted; determining the mood was far too serious, "Ted and I play this often, but I have to warn you...I'm pretty good!"

"Geez, I haven't played Scrabble in years...you two really do this often?" Judy looked surprised.

"Oh Yeah, we enjoy it. It stimulates our brains and forces us to actually talk and interact together...unlike just sitting watching T.V. like couch potatoes!" Jessica quickly set up the board.

As they played the game together, Judy could see the closeness between Jessica and Ted. They had been married for nearly thirty years and were high school sweethearts before that. The love they had for each other filled the room. Oh, how she longed for that love in her life. How she missed loving someone and caring for them.

How she loved making a man happy. She thought about these things as she sipped her tea and tried her best to put the longest most sensible words together that she could; however, Jessica retained her Scrabble championship.

When Judy went to bed that night, in the guest room up stairs, she thought about Jim; his smile, his sensitivity and wondered if they would see each other again sometime. She wondered how he would match up to her list she was working on of requirements for a man. From what she knew of him he was doing pretty well. But she didn't know him that well, and would soon find out that what he wanted wasn't what she wanted.

Chapter 4
Visiting Family

"Are we there yet?" Alex asked for the hundredth time in an hour.

"NOT YET!" both Alicia and Judy answered together.

It was a long drive from Harvey, Nebraska to Worthington, Colorado where Judy's parents lived in their little retirement complex. The kids had been really good traveling for the most part. Of course having a portable T.V. with videos helped. Alicia wouldn't have it any other way. She did not have the patience her mother had when it came to kids.

They had stopped along the way in Keller, Nebraska to visit a tourist attraction, but when they arrived it was closed so they went to an amusement center instead. It was an awesome place with games of all kinds and activities for the kids.

Neither Alicia nor Judy had a lot of money, but they had saved a little for this trip. Some of the financial burden had been lifted from Judy since she filed for bankruptcy. There was just no way she was going to be able to get on top of her debt. Fighting her debt was so frustrating for her. That's why she was attracted to this one game in the fun center where they stopped with the kids.

Judy put on the electronic gloves and went up against various opponents in an electronic boxing match. It was invigorating to knock out those guys. Every frustration and aggravation she ever had was released during those matches and the grandkids enjoyed cheering Grandma on to victory.

Soon it was time to get back on the road. There were still a lot of miles to cover.

"Just one more game, Grandma...please!" Alex and Maggie Lu pleaded. As they went out the door there was a dollar crane game.

Judy gave each of the grandkids a dollar to try their luck at manipulating the wobbly crane over the assortment of stuffed animals and other gadgets; then strategically drop the crane's opened jaws down in an attempt to capture a coveted prize.

Of course Alicia had to help Maggie Lu since she was so little. Usually the crane would mysteriously let go just as the object is lifted out of place, but to their amazement, each of them came up with a nice stuffed animal to cuddle with on the rest of the trip. It was a fun time for all.

Darkness had set in when they arrived in Worthington, but the drive was a familiar one. Judy and her family had lived in Bellington, just north of her parents, for seven years. It was one of the twenty-two moves she and Lenny had done during marriage. He probably never would have left Colorado if she hadn't forced the move. Judy wanted a simpler life and hated the congestion of the city. They were from small towns in Nebraska and she wanted to go back; believing it was what their family needed.

Colorado and the city held the painful memory of the loss of their youngest child, Miranda. She was only thirteen years old when she died. The loss of her weighed heavy on Judy's heart. Miranda had taken her bicycle to visit her friend who lived on the other side of Bellington. She had made the familiar ride many times before. The day she left, Judy felt uneasy and expressed her feelings to Miranda, but she was always so independent and stubborn.

She was angry when she told Judy, "I am not going to have you drive me to Natalie's house, mother! I am perfectly capable of riding there myself...I've done it a hundred times! You are too paranoid with your stupid premonition feelings! Just leave me alone!"

They argued, she left and never came home. She had to cross a busy street during rush hour. It was an accident. The driver didn't see her come up beside him as he made the turn. Judy often wondered if her sweet Miranda was still angry with her in heaven. Lenny blamed Judy for the accident. He said she should have been firmer with their daughter. He didn't discuss it any further. She thought, maybe, back in Nebraska the family would find the happiness they were forever searching for, but happiness wasn't in Nebraska for them either.

Now Judy's parents lived in Colorado and she was visiting them.

"Hi, Itty Bitty Buddies!" a familiar voice called through the darkness.

"Great Papa!" Alex and Maggie Lu shouted together with excitement and they went running toward him.

"Be careful with him!" Judy warned her grandchildren, "Hi, Dad...we're finally here."

"How was the drive? Did you get pretty good gas mileage?" Dad asked. He was always concerned about the price of gas. Judy laughed at the thought that he would probably drive 10 miles to save a penny a gallon.

"We did ok, Dad. The drive was fine. How's Momma?"

"Oh she's ok...tired. She's inside and anxious to see you. Let me help you with your things." As he picked up a suitcase and held onto Maggie Lu's hand he led the way to their apartment.

Judy's mom, Bonnie, was sitting in her rocker by the window anxiously waiting for her visitors to come in. As they opened the door Sparky, their little old, nearly blind, terrier barked happily.

"Oh Dottie would have loved to visit you, but we left her with some friends back home. Sorry about that buddy." Judy patted his head.

"Great Nana!" The kids said and went over to get their hugs. They gently hugged back because they knew Great Nana was fragile and they had to be careful.

"How are you doing, Mom?" Judy asked, "You look good today. Your color is good."

"Today is a good day," she replied, "I'm so glad you are here. Come here Alicia and give me a hug. You look so beautiful. I like the color of your hair...something new?"

"You know me, Grandma...I'm always experimenting!" Alicia said as she brushed her fingers through her auburn locks.

"It looks good with your beautiful blue eyes," Grandma added, cupping Alicia's face in her hands and kissing her cheek.

"Mommy has blue eyes like me!" Maggie Lu's little voice chirped from below.

"And Great Nana has blue eyes like us, too!" Alicia added, lifting Maggie Lu in her arms.

Judy carefully scanned the room to get an idea of how her parents were caring for themselves. Everything seemed to be in order except for the little bags of coffee she spotted here and there. They were those bags like tea bags...for individual cups.

"Mom, why do you have coffee bags around the room?" she asked.

"Well, it's to cover up the other smells that seem to bother me. The smell of coffee doesn't bother me, so I put them out. It seems to help," her mother answered, plainly.

"Oh...okay...whatever works, Momma." And she kissed her on the cheek.

Judy's mother had emphysema and her breathing was often inhibited by various odors or chemicals that she seemed to detect even when no one else could. Whether or not it was actually medically verifiable or not, it was very real to her, and the family usually went along with it. Everywhere she went she had her little buddy oxygen tank with her to help her breath.

Judy enjoyed seeing her parents again. Bart and Bonnie Williams grew up together in the small town of Briarwood, Nebraska. Although he was several years older than she was, they eventually fell in love and married.

There's was a strong love and one that Judy had longed for all her life. She thought that was what she would always have someday; a husband who was caring and kind like her father. How on earth she ended up in the relationships she had was a mystery to her and one she vowed to never repeat.

"I hear you have met someone, Judy. Is he a nice man?" Bonnie asked her daughter while getting some cookies out for the children.

They were those pink wafer cookies with icing in between the layers. Judy remembered eating those as a young girl and reached for one while responding to her mother's curiosity, "He's just a friend, Mom...that's all. He seems nice, but there's just something about him...I don't know..."

"He's odd!" Alicia butted in, "Admit it Mom, he's odd. It's like he's just too nice or something. I just hope you don't get too serious with him, because I think he's a little strange."

"We just enjoy each other's company. He has a great smile and he is a good father," Judy stated in Jim's defense.

"Oh, he has children?" Judy's dad, Bart, joined in, "What happened to his wife? What does he do for a living?"

"He is divorced...actually he is twice divorced. He remarried shortly after is first divorce but it didn't work out. He is a mail carrier in Shilo," Judy explained.

"Hmmmm...twice divorced, huh? There must be some kind of problem!" Bart scoffed.

"That's what I think!" Alicia piped in.

"Ok, listen...I'm divorced...Alicia, you're divorced...and twice, too, I might add...would you want people to think these things about you?" Judy fired back.

"You know...we all have our problems..." Bonnie calmly and meekly interceded, "You know what they say about glass houses...if you live in one don't throw stones! I'm glad you have someone to go out with once in a while. You're a smart girl, Judy, and you've been through some difficult times, but you've learned from them and I'm sure you will proceed with caution this time. When the right man comes into your life...you'll know." Bonnie was always the peace maker in the family.

"Thanks, Mom" Judy sipped her coffee not sure if she was as smart as her mother gave her credit for. Jim was a nice guy, but terrified of commitment to any kind of relationship other than "friends" but he wanted the "perks" of a serious relationship that involves a commitment.

It was confusing for Judy and went against her re-established conscience to do otherwise. She enjoyed having the companionship, but knew the relationship would never amount to anything. It seemed as if she was just wasting her time and she often felt a little "used". The real surprise was when he told her he had another woman in his life. She was a much younger woman…a college student. Apparently, they dated and she ended the relationship when she went back to school.

"I just can't seem to get her out of my head and I think of her often," he told Judy one evening during what should have been their intimate moment.

"Do you still see each other or stay in touch?" Judy asked.

"We call each other…occasionally," he responded.

Judy wasn't sure what to make of it. He seemed to want his cake and eat it too and she told him so. This time away was a good thing. She needed time to refocus and be with her family. She added to her list "NOT AFRAID TO COMMIT!" as a priority for her "dream guy."

"When are we going to Casa Bonita?" Alex called out, watching a commercial of the restaurant on the T.V.

Casa Bonita was a fantastic place in Denver to take kids. It had pink stucco on the outside and inside was like another world. You would think you were outside in Mexico in a beautiful courtyard restaurant. There were flowers and waterfalls and best of all the cliff divers. The food wasn't that great, but the atmosphere was incredible. Every visit to the folks involved a trip to Casa Bonita.

Judy sat down near her grandchildren and said, "We'll go there tomorrow. So you two need to get a good rest tonight. Let's get your bed set up here on the floor and get you tucked in…give Nana and Papa kisses good night."

Alex and Maggie Lu raced over to their great grandparents, "'Night Great Nana, 'night Great Papa…"

And then little Maggie Lu asked innocently, "Are you going with us tomorrow to the pink castle?"

Bonnie hugged her softly and said, "No dear, not this time. We'll just wait here for you to come back and tell us all about your adventures. You be sure to eat some of those honey and bread treats for me!"

"Oh, I will…lots of them!" Maggie Lu responded.

"Me too…I bet I eat more than you Mag-pie!" Alex teased. And they all laughed.

In no time at all, the children were asleep and the adults continued their conversation around the table. Bonnie was getting weary and occasionally her eyes would close and her head would bob downward nearly hitting the table before she would jolt awake once more.

"Do you need to go to bed, Mom?" Judy asked.

"No, no…I'm fine…it's just the medication. It makes me so groggy. I do this all the time" her mother responded as her father nodded his head in agreement.

"Grandma, you really do look good, though. They must be treating you okay. Are you feeling any stronger?" Alicia gently placed her hand over the tiny frail hand of her grandmother.

"I have good days and bad days" Bonnie replied giving Alicia's hand a loving squeeze.

"Mom says you made a new clown outfit. Can I see it?" Alicia asked, trying to defer the topic to something more positive.

"Oh it's put away in the other room; perhaps tomorrow. I'll try and locate it while you are out, okay?" Bonnie didn't have the energy to go look for it that night. But she smiled lovingly at Alicia…her very first grandchild.

"That's fine, Grandma…anytime. I suppose I should hit the hay, too. So I have the energy tomorrow to keep up with those two," Alicia said, nodding toward her little ones asleep on the floor with good old Sparky. "Are you coming, Mom?" Alicia asked, making her way to the tiny guest room.

"I'll be there in a minute," Judy responded, knowing her dad could really use her help encouraging her mom to go to bed. "Let me help you, Mom," Judy said, carefully assisting her mom from her chair, "You and Dad have a good night's rest. We'll see you in the morning."

"Well, I guess I could sleep," Bonnie replied, trying to convince herself. She just hadn't slept well since the last visit to the doctor. The thought of not having much time left makes one feel that sleep is wasting it away. She wanted to reap every moment for all those last minute thoughts and prayers. She felt as if her life was like sand running through the hour glass. There was no stopping it now...no more chances for delays. Her time would soon be up and she knew it...Bart knew it, too...and they were just trying to live in spite of it. She wondered if her children knew it.

"God bless you", she whispered to her family as she joined her husband in their room. Then she tenderly blew them all kisses.

"It was soooo fun!" Maggie Lu shrieked as she entered Bart and Bonnie's apartment. "The men jumped into the water from high up! And...and...there was this big, huge monkey...and...I was scared!" Maggie Lu's eyes were wide with excitement, "You should have seen it, Great Nana!"

"Oh, I know...I've seen it before. Sounds like you had a lot of fun!" And she gave her great-granddaughter a hug.

"Mom, where do you want to put this box of pictures?" a familiar voice sounded from the bedroom.

"Hey, Shirley! How are you?" Judy greeted her sister.

"Aunt Shirley! Aunt Shirley!" Maggie Lu and Alex ran up to their favorite aunt, hugging her waist.

"Hi kiddos, so you did the Casa Bonita thing again, huh?' she said, directing a wink toward Judy.

"Oh yeah, can't come out here without making that ritual! Is Terry with you?" Judy asked.

"Not this time. He sends his greetings though. He had to go run some errands for his folks. This is what we do on most of our weekends!" Shirley said with a smile, "How long are you staying?"

"This is just one of those quick trips" Judy explained, "Alicia and I both have to get back to work the day after tomorrow and the kids have school. I left my little dog with friends and I'm sure she's wondering when I'll return, too. Mom and Dad really wanted us to come visit, so we just made the drive."

"I'm glad you came. Have you talked to the folks much?" Shirley asked as Judy helped her lift the heavy box of pictures onto the closet shelf.

"Not too much. Do you think they are telling us all they know about Mom's condition? I just have a feeling they are holding something back," Judy said.

"I'm sure they are telling us all they want us to know. I've tried to find out more information but maybe not knowing is better for us. I just feel we need to enjoy the time we have…and that is what Mom and Dad seem to want too." Shirley was not only older but often wiser, too.

"Well, I'm beat. I just want to sit and enjoy our time with everyone here. I do have one place I need to visit before I go back. We'll go there this afternoon." Judy stated quietly.

Shirley gave her little sister an understanding hug. "I go there for you when I can. She was my godchild you know." Her eyes filled with tears as she shook her head back briskly and said, "We live for today…let's make it the best day we can!"

The sky was becoming cloudy as Judy, Alicia and the two children walked up the steep sidewalk to the large pine tree ahead.

"Just a little further," Judy coaxed them, "I can see the wind chime on the branch that we left for her on the last visit. Do you see it Maggie Lu?" she said, pointing toward the tree.

"I see it…I hear it!" Maggie Lu ran ahead with excitement as Alicia held tightly to her mother's arm.

"I love you, Mom," She whispered softly, "I know this is hard for you…it's hard for all of us." A tear trickled down her cheek as she brushed it away with her finger tips. Alex walked slowly behind them, thinking quietly to himself.

Soon they were there. It was a beautiful spot high on a hill in the shade of a Ponderosa Pine tree. The cool Colorado breezes made the chimes sing mystically, communicating with the wind and the spirits surrounding the grounds around them. In front of them was the little stone with an angel perched on top of it to one side. The angel was blowing a kiss, just like Judy had seen her mother do the night before. The writing on the stone read:

Miranda Lynn Braxtin
February 16, 1979 - September 17, 1992
"Rest peacefully, Jesus holds you now"

Tenderly Judy knelt beside the little marker and brushed the pine needles from the cold stone; her fingers touched each letter as if to evoke every beautiful thought and memory of her little girl; including the nights of reading to her from a little book Judy had written and illustrated to give her peace before going to sleep.

The book told a story of a little girl, Miranda, who saw Jesus talking to some children. The little girl ran up to him and he lifted her into his arms. The little girl felt so loved and safe and he told her he was always with her and she never had to be afraid. Judy read her that story nearly every night.

"You were so beautiful," she thought, silently to herself, the tears filling her eyes, "So beautiful and so stubborn and I miss you…Jesus holds you now."

Silently she sat there remembering, longing and pleading with God to forgive her. She still blamed herself for the accident that day. If she had only been more firm…if she had taken her feelings more seriously and not discredited them or tried to ignore them. If only…

"I like the angel," Maggie Lu's little voice interrupted her thoughts, "She is blowing a kiss like Great Nana does. I like her…I think Aunt Miranda likes her sitting on top of her here, in this place, watching over her…don't you?"

Everyone laughed. "Yes, I think you're right. Miranda does like having her angel sitting on top of her watching over her...you're so right little one!" And Judy hugged her tightly.

"I wish I had known her," Alex remarked, staring blankly at the stone, "I think she would have been a fun Aunt to have...from the stories Mom has told me."

"She was fun, Alex, and you would have enjoyed her. She loved kids and often babysat for others. She was smart, and feisty, and so independent. I think she knows who you are and she loves you." Judy hugged Alex close.

"Me too? Does she know me and love me too?" Maggie Lu asks.

Alicia picked up her little girl and said, "You too, honey...she loves all of us." Then she put her arm around her mother with an assuring hug.

Saying good-bye is never easy. There is never enough time to do or say all the things you want to.

"Oh, Grandma, I didn't get to see your new clown suit!" Alicia said sadly.

"Maybe next time," Bonnie answered with a gentle smile, "Maybe next time." And Bart put his arm gently around her small shoulders expressing his love and protection.

As Judy loaded the last of the luggage in the car she glanced over to her aging parents, with their arms joined together, standing on the sidewalk, in front of the car. "Why can't I be so lucky? Why can't I have a love like that?" She pondered and smiled at them both. "Well, I guess we're on our way!" she said, slowly approaching them.

Instinctively her mother reached out to her, drew her near, and with shortened breath said, "Thank you for coming, Judy. I love you. You be careful now. Remember, faith and hope are the wings we soar with. God bless you."

"I love you, Momma...God bless you too." As Judy hugged her little mother close and kissed her.

"Hey, I need one of those, too!" Bart playfully demanded; putting his free arm around Judy giving her a huge hug and kissing her on the forehead.

"I love you too, Dad. Take good care of Mom and yourself. Don't get too worn down. Let me know if there is anything I can do," Judy gently instructed her father.

"I will. Call us when you get home, so we don't have to worry, okay? Did you check the oil? The tires look okay. Do you have a full tank of gas?" It was his usual good bye speech.

"Grandpa, I checked everything...don't worry!" Alicia joined in, "We'll call you tonight."

"Bye Great Nana and Papa!" Alex and Maggie Lu cried out from the back seat, "We love you!"

"God bless you!" Maggie Lu added waving frantically as she blew kisses out the window.

"God bless you, too...all of you." Bonnie said with tears in her eyes and blowing her kisses back. Then the car drove away.

Chapter 5
Who Blew Out the Light?

It was summertime and getting really miserable in the lab. Judy had reached the end of her endurance when she confronted Ray.

"Either you do something about this damn air conditioner in here or I'm out of here! It is ninety-eight degrees inside the lab and I can barely function! There is no ventilation and the clones are dying off! All the work I have done these past months is dying! Do you hear me…ENOUGH! Do something about these deplorable conditions!"

Ray looked shocked as Judy stomped away. The greenhouse workers shot glances back and forth among themselves as she past them by.

She needed some air! It was time for a walk around the park. Inside the greenhouses the temperature had reached 110 degrees!

"This is ridiculous!" She said to herself as she started her familiar walk around the park. "Judy, you can do better than this, for Pete's sake. Why put yourself through this aggravation! You are smarter than this," She continued.

Then suddenly as if a light went on inside her head, she remembered the information she had received from the Community College in Northtown. "Tomorrow I am going to go talk to someone there. I need to continue my education and find a new direction. There has to be something I can do. There must be someway I can use my abilities and talents to earn a reasonable living. I just need some direction and to refine my skills. I'll do it!"

She took the rest of the day off and called it a "mental health day". Summertime in Northeast Nebraska means plenty of activities. There were county fairs every weekend and street dances, too. It was hot, humid and buggy.

"I'm like a mosquito magnet!" Judy said as she lathered on the repellent. She was manning a face painting booth at the local county fair. Something she had done for several years and looked forward to so much.

She loved working with the kids and enjoyed drawing the characters or designs on their little faces. Sometimes she would even do some for adults on their arms or shoulders. The mosquitoes were terrible that night. She always used repellant, but this time forgot to put it on her feet. They bit her repeatedly before she realized it.

"You want a beer?" Jim asked, as he leaned over the fence from the beer garden. His voice was a little more distant than usual.

"He must have read my letter." Judy thought as she shook her head no and replied, "Not just yet. Maybe later."

"Okay, talk to you later," Jim said as he joined his Shilo buddies at a table.

Judy had sent him a letter agreeing with him that they should just remain friends and nothing more. She stated that she was not prepared to get involved in a relationship with someone who wasn't able to make a commitment. She went on to tell him that he is a really nice guy and that she hoped he figured out what it is he wants someday.

It was obvious he had read the letter. Even though it stated back to him what he had been saying to her all along, it was as if once he realized she wasn't going to "chase" after him he was disappointed. "Alicia was right…he is different," she thought to herself. She wouldn't hear from him for two weeks.

At the Steam Horse Restaurant in Hopstown Judy glanced around the table and said, "I got approved for my financial aid today."

"Judy is taking some classes at the College in Northtown?" Jim said as he looked up from his supper. They were out on a weekend "friendly date" with some of his friends from Shilo.

"I think it's a *wonderful* idea." He added, in his strangely high pitched tone. He didn't mean to, but he was beginning to irritate her.

"What are you interested in studying, Judy?" Arlene asked, as she took a sip from her beer.

"I'm not sure. I know I don't want to do anything in the medical field, but I would like to somehow make a difference in people's lives. I love writing and enjoy painting and drawing. I have been trying to get some children's books published for sometime now. Maybe I'll go and try to learn how to market myself as a writer and illustrator." Judy responded, trying to show confidence, but lacking it terribly.

"Do you think there is any *real* money in that? I mean…is it very stable? It seems to me the competition is pretty tough. Why don't you go into some area of computer work? That seems to be where the jobs are." Arlene was a true left brain person; very analytical, punctual and concise.

Judy smiled back and said, "Thanks, Arlene. I'll have to check into that." Then she thought, "What am I doing here?"

Jim smiled from across the table. "And what am I doing with him? He runs so hot and cold I never know what to expect. Sometimes we can have so much fun together. He loves to dance…but…oh, man…why do my eyes hurt so bad!" Judy had a dull aching pain behind her eyes. "I feel like crap tonight. And my skin hurts. I need to just get out of here and go home to bed…something is wrong, I can tell." She managed to get through the meal.

"You want to come in and watch some T.V.?" Jim asked politely and smiling as they exited his car.

"You know…I would…but I just don't feel well…I think I need to go home and get some rest. Thanks anyway." And she kissed Jim on the cheek concerned about passing her illness to him.

"I'll try and call you tomorrow," Jim said he walked her to her car parked in the street by his house.

"Yeah, ok...that's fine...goodnight, Jim," Judy said as she fumbled for her keys. Her head felt like it was going to explode. "I just need sleep..." she mumbled to herself.

When she got home she collapsed in her bed with Dottie snuggled in beside her. All night long she would wake up in sweats, but unable to move or get up. The next day she felt better but so tired. There were strange itchy bumps on her arms.

"These look like hives, but not like any I've had before," Judy said to herself, as she rubbed hydrocortisone cream on her arms to sooth the itch; remembering the time she broke out in hives in Cancun, Mexico from severe sunburn. There was also the time she had shingles when she was married to Lenny and they moved abruptly. This rash wasn't like those times though. Maybe she was just nervous about the changes she was making in her life.

The first day of school! How exciting it was to walk onto the campus and frantically search for her classes. What ever it was that got her down over the weekend seemed to be passing. It should be gone...she just about slept all weekend. The rash was still on her arms and she was still so tired. But nothing was going to keep her from her dream of finally going to college.

She had arranged her schedule at work so that she would put in thirty-two hours in order to maintain her full time status and benefits and still be able to carry a full load for her college credits. Her financial aid would pay for her classes and books as well as provide extra income for gas and expenses. It was a perfect plan...or so she thought.

"Ray, this is Judy. Listen, I'm not going to come into the lab today. I'm at school, but I noticed I have this peculiar rash on my arms and I think I should go to the doctor and have it checked out. No...I don't have a doctor here yet so I'm going to one in Fairway where I used to live. I don't know when I'll get back, but its seventy-five miles from here so it won't be today. Yeah, I'll let you know. Bye."

As she drove, she wondered what the doctor would find out. She knew her body well enough to know that something just wasn't right. Could it be West Nile? The drive from Northtown to her doctor in Fairway seemed particularly long.

"I'm so tired! I don't know if I will make it...maybe some coffee...I'll stop here," she said as she pulled into the station, "Hopefully this will give me some energy and help me stay awake."

Arriving at the clinic, she peeked around the corner of the receptionist area, "Hello, Carol," she said to her good friend working at the desk.

"Well, Judy! What a surprise...what are you doing here?" Carol asked.

"I'm not feeling well...I called in...I need Dr. Christian to check me out," Judy said weakly.

"I just need to update some information, Judy. I'm sorry you're ill. It won't be long and Doctor will see you. How have you been otherwise?" Carol handed the clipboard to Judy.

"I started college...as a matter of fact today was my first day...and my job is good. I'm doing much better, thanks...just need to get over this bug." Judy sat and started filling out the information and handed Carol her insurance card.

"I think of you often...and I miss seeing you," Carol said softly. "It's not the same without you around," she added while Judy returned the smile.

Carol and her husband Dan had also traveled occasionally with Judy and Dr. Dickhead to Mexico and Europe. The four of them had quite a time together, although Judy and Carol spent most of the time dealing with their partner's drunken attitudes.

Carol returned a knowing smile back.

As Judy sat waiting to be called back to the patient area, she tried to recall just when and where she met up with the mosquito that could have infected her. Living in Northeast Nebraska, dealing with the ever-present mosquito population is a normal event during the summer months. Every Wednesday evening the truck with the mosquito fogger would go rambling down the alley behind her house. This event took place in most of the towns.

Judy thought to herself, "Could the encounter have occurred when I was visiting friends who lived along the river? Or maybe when I was at work? I remember one very large mosquito bite I had on my chest that just didn't seem to want to heal. I even remember thinking that it would be just my luck I'd come down with West Nile! Oh, my gosh! There was the weekend at the county fair! I was bitten all those times on my feet...how could I be so careless?"

"Judy?" A woman in brightly colored scrubs asked as she held open the door.

Judy shifted her attention to the assistant, "Yes?"

The assistant said, "Doctor will see you now."

Judy was escorted to the back area of the clinic where she was weighed and then asked to wait in the examination room. As the assistant took Judy's temperature and blood pressure she said, "Dr. Christian will be in to see you shortly."

"I am so sleepy!" Judy said to herself as she climbed up on the examination table, "Maybe I can just take a little nap here while I am waiting..." And within seconds she was sound asleep.

"So, you haven't been feeling so well?" Dr. Christian asked as he quietly opened the door. He had such a gentle and reassuring smile. "What seems to be the problem?"

"I don't know Doctor. I'm so tired and I have this strange rash on my arms and part of my body, but it doesn't really itch. My eyes hurt...behind the eyeballs...I'm just so tired!" Judy wearily replied.

"Any coughing...sore throat...neck stiffness?" he asked calmly as he listened to her chest and examined her neck, throat and ears.

"No...not really. The other night though I think I may have had a fever during the night. I was sweating profusely and couldn't get up," Judy recalled.

"Lay back on the table, please. I want to check your abdomen." Judy lay back down on the examination table as Dr. Christian probed around her belly, then took each leg and raised it checking for any pain.

"The symptoms you are experiencing could be attributed to several causes. I'm going to run some tests for strep throat. Mononucleosis and I also want to check you for the West Nile Virus.

We'll do a urinalysis and full blood work-up on you. Just wait here and the nurse will be right in." He gently patted Judy on the leg. "We'll find out what the problem is. The tests results should come back in a few days; however, the West Nile test takes one to two weeks. Once we get the tests back then I will determine how to proceed with the treatment plan. In the meantime, I want you to get plenty of rest, drink lots of fluids and take ibuprofen as needed for aches and pains. The nurse will bring in some samples of some cream for you to use on the rash." Then he added sternly, "Now, Judy, I want you to call immediately if you start to feel any worse, run a fever again, experience any pain or stiffness in your neck, or get a severe headache. Do you understand?"

"Yes, Doctor…I do…I will…thank you," Judy obediently replied.

As the nurse struggled to find a decent vein to draw blood from Judy's arm, the thoughts of what Dr. Christian had said kept spinning through her mind. "What on earth is wrong with me?" she thought.

By this time she was so tired she felt numb. "I just want to go home and go to bed…but I have such a long drive…maybe if I try and eat something…but I'm just not hungry."

"Doctor will call you when the tests come back. He'll want to see you again, then, I'm sure. I'm so sorry you're feeling so bad, Judy," Carol said as Judy stopped at her desk before leaving the clinic, "It was good seeing you again. Did…Have you…has Roger tried to call you?" She just had to know.

Judy looked wearily at her friend, not really wanting to discuss him at this time. "He called once to threaten me…that's all. But its ok, Carol. I don't care if I ever see him again or talk to him. He means nothing to me. And I told him so that day."

Carol looked surprised. "Oh, well, that's good…I guess. I haven't really seen him, but of course Dan has, since they hang out at the same places…you know."

Judy just smiled. She knew because she used to hang out there, too…enabling Dr. Dickhead to drink himself to oblivion and getting him home safely. What a crazy life…but it wasn't hers anymore. "I'll see you again, Carol. You take care…I need to make the drive home."

"Be careful, Judy." And out the doors Judy went.

As she got in her car she decided to give Brad a call and see if he wanted to meet her for a bite to eat. "Hi Brad, its Mom…are you busy?" she asked.

"No, not really…are you ok?" He could hear a difference in his mother's voice and he was concerned.

"I'm ok, I had a doctor's appointment here, but I need to get a bite to eat…want to meet me at Charlie & Pete's restaurant? I could go for their potato nachos." She tried to sound enthused.

"Sure, I'll meet you there. Sounds good. See you there." Brad was glad to have an excuse to get out of the house for a while.

The food just didn't taste good. Judy normally loved to eat and especially potato nachos, but for some reason she wasn't hungry.

"Are you feeling ok, mom?" Brad asked.

"No, not really. Dr. Christian is running some tests. I won't know what it is for a while," Judy said as she sipped her soda.

"What does he think it could be?" Brad continued nibbling on his mother's nachos.

"They're checking me for several things…even West Nile…but that is so rare, I'm sure it isn't that…I just feel so terrible and sleepy. I really should head back and go to bed." Judy tried to minimize her concern so not to worry her son.

"It was good seeing you again, Mom. Jen and I will try to get up to see you soon, okay?"

"That would be fine. Thanks for joining me. Tell Jen and the kids hi from me." Judy reached up and hugged her, now big, little boy. He had the physique of his father, maybe even larger. He was a big man, not fat, by any means just tall and strong. He started out big at over nine pounds and nearly two feet long at birth. He waved as she drove away.

For the next week Judy continued going to class as scheduled. Her mornings seemed better than the later part of the day. Occasionally she experienced nausea that was very similar to morning sickness. Her throat did get sore and it felt like someone had their hand around her neck. There was a lot of pressure in her neck and ears, probably due to the swollen glands. Her tongue felt like it was coated and she couldn't taste much of anything. The rash was starting to fade. Occasionally she would have an itchy spot that would flair up.

She learned quickly that when she felt tired she had to sleep. She would go to work and go to classes, go home, study for an hour to an hour and a half, eat some soup, drink some orange juice, and then go to bed. There wasn't any energy left for her to do anything else. She didn't have an appetite, but she ate chicken noodle soup and she craved orange juice and drank it by the gallons. She added a Zinc supplement to her diet and drank Echinacea tea.

Before she was sick she walked about two miles a day, but she used all her energy now just to focus on her studies and do her job in the lab. There were days in the lab that she had to leave early in order to sleep. She even fell asleep behind the hood working occasionally. Her missed work put a strain on her finances.

"Hi, Sue, this is Judy Braxtin. I was wondering if you got any results back on my tests?" Judy asked the nurse at Dr. Christian's office.

"Well, the mono and strep are negative, but your white blood count was low which indicates your body is probably fighting a virus of some kind. We haven't received the results of the West Nile Virus test yet. We'll call you as soon as we hear. How are you doing?" Sue asked with concern.

"I'm trying to reserve my strength for what I have to do. I'm just so tired and I don't have much of an appetite. I just eat soup and drink orange juice," Judy said.

"Sounds like you are doing what you need to, Judy. You be sure to call us if you start feeling worse or if you run fever or get a severe headache, okay?"

"I will. Thanks, Sue. Call me when the test results come in. Bye."

A week had passed. It was Thursday, September 4, 2003, as Judy drove the familiar highway to Northtown Community College for her morning classes. The DJ on KPGY announced that Nebraska was the leading state in the nation for deaths due to the West Nile Virus. Normally this information would have gone into one ear and out the other without much thought, but that morning it hit Judy in the stomach like a strong punch. Her eyes began to tear as she wondered what was ahead for her. Just yesterday she had received the news that her blood test, from the doctor's visit one week ago, had come back positive for this same virus

"Now what do I do, Sue?" Judy had pleaded with Dr. Christian's nurse for the right answers.

"Just keep doing what you have been. Increase your vitamin C and drink plenty of liquids. Doctor will want to see you again to go over some things with you. You have to make sure you get enough rest. We'll see you at your next appointment. Judy, you take care now and call if your symptoms get worse."

The first thing Judy decided she needed to do after learning she had contracted the West Nile Virus was to inform her employer. She wanted them to know why she wasn't able to work as many hours as she originally thought she would and why she needed to take time off for doctor's appointments. Fortunately, her supervisors at the nursery were very understanding of the circumstances. Judy had heard of others suffering with the disease whose employers questioned the legitimacy of their symptoms.

There were mornings when Judy would wake up feeling so good. "Maybe it's gone?" She'd think and then about mid-day the incredible fatigue would come over her and she would need to immediately lie down and sleep. When she slept she would dream bizarre dreams. Talking with others with the virus, she learned they would do the same.

"What is wrong with me?" Judy said to herself in total frustration. "I know this! Why can't I think of how to do it?"

Her mind wasn't doing what she wanted it to. She experienced lapses in memory and couldn't always focus clearly. She had to really slow herself down to keep from making crucial errors in the lab. This increased with added stress or fatigue.

The success of her job depended on her ability to maintain sterile plant transfers and it was easy to contaminate the cultures if she was not very careful. She kept a daily checklist and log to verify what she did every day and needed to do.

After informing her employer, Judy also shared her condition with each of her instructors at the college. Fortunately, because of the heavy media coverage, most of them were very aware of the Virus and expressed concern. They were very helpful and understanding when her symptoms created problems with her required work.

"This is so strange." Judy thought to herself as she stared at the exam before her. "The words are jumping all over the page! I can't tell where the answer box is on the card! Focus, Judy! Make your mind focus!"

But it was no use. She did the best she could but she knew it was disastrous. She had never experienced anything like it before.

"Are you all right?" Ms. Tomlinson asked as Judy placed her exam on the desk at the front of the room.

"No...I don't think so...I think I really bombed this exam...I couldn't see it right. The words were all over the page," Judy explained to her instructor.

"Listen, don't be concerned about it. You are allowed to "throw out" a grade this term if it's bad. Maybe you need to take your exams isolated, where there is less distraction and stress. I can arrange for that if you think it would help." Ms. Tomlinson was a considerate instructor and she and Judy got along very well.

"That would be great if it is possible...I mean it is certainly worth a try. It was the weirdest thing! Thank you for understanding."

"Listen, Judy, I know how hard you are trying and you are an excellent student. I want you to succeed at your goals. You'll get through this, you'll see."

"I hope so...thanks." Judy felt somewhat better, but aggravated that she needed special concern and treatment. She didn't like drawing attention to herself.

"I hate this!" Judy exclaimed in exasperation, "Who blew out my light!"

That was just how she felt. As if the light inside her that gave her life, joy, and energy was suddenly snuffed out or barely burning.

Every decision she made was based on whether or not she had enough energy left to follow through. She learned to deal with the fatigue...she just got more rest. She adjusted to the way her mind had changed by staying calm and focused. She controlled her aching joints and muscles with medication and the ever-present sore throat, occasional ear aches and numbness on her face became the norm for her. What she missed most of all was that light inside of her; that incredible energy she used to have. She wanted it back and wondered if it would ever return.

There were no clear cut answers to her questions as to how long she would feel this way and if there would be residual effects from this virus that invaded her body, mind, and soul. The only consolation was in talking with others with the same virus.

As bad as it was, she was more fortunate than many who had been infected; some were paralyzed and many had died. Although there were over two-thousand people infected that year, the others to talk to were still few and far between.

Through research Judy learned that there were some in other states who had contracted the virus two years before and were still experiencing symptoms from it. The doctor said she would get better, but could not give her any definition on when or how much better she would feel. He couldn't guarantee she wouldn't get worse. It was frustrating! It seemed that everyday there was another person who died from the Virus. Usually they were older, but not always.

"Hi Momma..." Judy's voice was hesitant. It was time to tell her parents about the disease. "What's wrong, Judy? Has something happened?" Bonnie was concerned.

"No...well...yes...I mean I haven't been feeling well...and I need to tell you that I found out I have West Nile...but I'm ok, Momma...really I am."

"Oh, no...that isn't good...people are dying from that...are you sure you're okay?" she responded.

"Yes, Momma. I am just really tired most of the time. And I don't have a lot of energy…I can really relate to how you feel, now," she said hoping to lighten things up.

"You need to be sure to take care of yourself, Judy. This is a very serious thing."

"Oh, I am Momma. I go to the doctor regularly. But there isn't a cure, you know…just treatment of the symptoms. They say I'll feel better eventually. They just don't know when. But I'm pacing myself and getting lots of rest. How are you doing?"

"Don't you worry about me. I'm fine…same old thing, but we manage. Daddy takes good care of me."

"I'm glad you have each other. Dottie takes care of me, too," Judy said teasing and laughing.

"Well, that's good…how is school going?" Bonnie inquired.

"It's good Mom, very challenging, but I love it. I am learning so much. Work is okay too. I did cut my hours back at the lab though."

"Just don't over do it with everything," Bonnie warned her daughter.

"Oh, I'm not. I'm careful. Alicia and Brad keep an eye out for me, too. I'll be fine. I just wanted to let you and Daddy know."

"We'll keep you in our prayers, honey."

"I know you will…I count on it, Momma…thank you. I'll call again soon. I need to take a nap before I study and have supper. You take care, too. And keep me informed of how you are. You know I keep you in my prayers, too…both of you…I love you."

"We love you, too, honey…God bless!"

As Judy hung up the phone she hung her head and cried. They were emotional tears, cleansing tears, tears of exhaustion. "It will get better…It has to," she cried.

Judy was awakened from a sound sleep by the ring of the telephone.

"Mom! The house is on fire! We're out…I called the fire department…please come!" It was Alicia and then the town fire whistle went off.

"I'll be right there!" Judy quickly hung up the phone and went to her car. Alicia's house was only a few blocks away but Judy wanted to get there quickly. "A fire...I wonder how? I hope they remembered to get Daisy out!" Daisy was Alicia's cocker spaniel.

When Judy arrived on the scene she could see the smoke seeping out of the closed upstairs window; an occasional flame dancing in the background. "What happened?" She asked as she approached her daughter. Daisy came up and greeted her.

"I don't know!" We just got home...I picked up the kids after work. The door was shut to the upstairs and when I opened it there was this glow at the top of the steps and this terrible heat! Then I realized there was a fire up there...I can't believe it! We weren't even home!" Alicia stood gazing at the upstairs window of her son's bedroom.

Harvey's volunteer fire department arrived and quickly hooked up the water hoses. They put on their oxygen equipment and masks and entered the house with the hose ready to blast the flames with water from the hydrant. Once upstairs they opened the hose and started dousing the flames.

The window was broken and smoldering debris was thrown out onto the ground below; a charred comforter, wet and blackened pillows, and the mattress which was nearly consumed from the fire. The firemen worked for over and hour putting water on the flames and the hot spots upstairs.

"Help! Get some help over here!" A fireman staggered out of the house, small flames coming from his hood and mask. Instantly his comrades were around him removing the debris that had lodged in his protective gear.

"I'm okay," he said as he removed his helmet, mask and hood; shaking his head and rubbing his hair briskly to make sure there wasn't residue left.

The upstairs was a total loss and there was smoke and water damage in the lower level also. Fortunately, Alicia had good renter's insurance which would cover and replace everything.

"Where are we going to live now, Grandma?" Little Maggie Lu wondered as she stared at the smoldering rubble along side their house.

"You'll stay with me," Judy assured her, "I'll clean out the studio room and you can sleep in there until your house is fixed up…or you get a different one. Don't worry little one, it will be okay."

"Daisy, too?" Maggie Lu asked as she sat on the grass petting her companion.

"Yes, Daisy, too," Judy replied and she hugged her daughter and grandson.

"What could have happened…" Alex wondered as he kicked the burned remains of his mattress with his shoe. "Why did we have to have a fire? And why was it in MY room!" He moaned.

"It will be all right, Alex. We can replace the things that you lost, but we can't replace a life. I'm just glad you are all okay, aren't you?" Judy put her arm around Alex's shoulders as he nodded, still gazing at the smoldering rubble before him.

Alicia starred at the house as a tear ran down her cheek. "I don't need this right now. Work is already upset with me for missing as much as I have. I just don't know how they'll be about all this."

"Listen, you have good insurance. It's just going to take some time. You can stay with me for as long as it takes. They'll understand at work…it was an accident."

Then Judy said, "I'll see if Jim can bring his truck up to move your bed and some things over to my house. I'm sure he will."

"That would be great if he would," Alicia said with a sigh, "What a mess! The water dripped through to the downstairs. Everything is so smoky and there is soot everywhere." Alicia was overwhelmed.

"It looks like the fire originated in the northeast bedroom upstairs," The fire chief explained to Alicia, "Looks like faulty wiring on a lamp that was next to the bed. The fire itself was contained to that room, but the heat and smoke went everywhere. There is quite a bit of damage. You say you have renter's insurance?"

"Yes…yes I do. When can we go inside?" Alicia asked, curious as to what "quite a bit of damage" might look like. "We'll need to get the bed out from the downstairs bedroom tonight…will that be ok?

"We're pretty certain we got all the hot spots, but we're going to keep an eye on it for a while. You can get the bed…but wait until tomorrow to go upstairs." And she thanked the chief as he walked away.

"Hi, Jim…sorry to bother you, but I have a favor to ask…" Judy began her telephone conversation she could almost feel the uncertainty on the other end of the line but she continued, "Alicia had a fire in her house today…"

"Oh, my! Is she okay?" Jim interrupted.

"Yes, she's fine…they're all fine…but they can't stay in the house until it is cleaned up. So they are staying with me for a while…" Judy still didn't finish her request before Jim interrupted.

"That's good that you live so close," he added.

"Yes…Yes…but we need to move some of her things and we don't have a truck. Could you bring your pick up here so we could load her bed and some things in it tonight?" There…she finished. It wasn't so hard to do after all.

"Tonight? Yeah…sure…I can do that," he was hesitant, but agreed.

"Thanks, Jim. I really appreciate it!" Judy said with relief.

"Hey, that's what friends are for…" Jim replied.

"Yeah, great…thanks again, Jim. See you soon." And they set the time. Judy laughed to herself at the fact that he had to throw the "friendship" factor in as a gentle reminder of what they are to each other.

Judy was exhausted by the time the room was set up and the kids were in bed. As she lay in bed with Dottie and Daisy now snuggled on top of the covers by her side, she prayed, "God, please help us…" And then she drifted off to sleep before any more of her prayer could be spoken.

Chapter 6
Endings and Beginnings

"Grandma! Grandma!" Maggie Lu was so excited as she greeted Judy at her car.

It had been a long day. Judy started the day early at the lab. She discovered that she was much more alert in the mornings and could get a lot of work done before heading to her classes at the community college. Wearily, she got out of the car.

"What is it little one?" she asked her overly excited grand daughter.

"We're going to Walt Disney World!" she said bursting with excitement. She could hardly contain herself.

"Oh really?" Judy answered looking up at Alicia as she walked toward them, "How's this going to happen?"

"Mom, I just decided. After moving and getting the things we needed, there was still a substantial amount of money left over from the insurance. I put it down on a planned trip for the four of us. You know we always talked about doing it someday...well, now is the time. If we don't do it now we probably never will." Alicia was determined. The decision was made.

"Can you...can we really afford to do this? When is this trip going to be?" Judy was concerned.

"No, we can't afford it, but we can't afford not to either. Life is too short...sometimes you just have to jump in. It isn't for four months yet...the beginning of February. It's a packaged deal. Everything is arranged. I put money down and we will make payments until it is paid for. It will be so fun, Mom! The kids are so excited!" Alicia hugged her mother trying to assure her.

"Ok, maybe you're right. I'm just really tired right now and need to take a quick nap before supper." Then she looked at Maggie Lu and said, "We're going to Disney World!" And she smiled.

"I think, maybe, we should stop seeing each other for a while," Jim said slowly holding Judy's hand as they sat out side his house. He had said this before and then he would call again.

"What is it you want, Jim? We've been doing this dating thing for six months now. Either it moves forward or it doesn't. I am not interested in just having someone to "hang out with" when ever it is convenient for you." Judy was getting frustrated with the uncertainty of their relationship.

"I know...I know...it's not you...it's me," Jim said whining, softly, taking the blame.

Judy felt he was trying to make her feel sorry for him or something. "Look, Jim, you know where I stand. I've tried to be honest with you from the beginning, but you are hard to figure out. Sometimes I think you want our relationship to move on beyond the friendship mode and then you pull back. I am not interested in doing the dating thing, especially dating a lot of people at once. I don't have the energy or the desire to do that."

"I know...I feel so bad telling you this now with you being sick and all. I feel like such a jerk!" Jim said emotionally. He seemed genuinely sorry for his indecisiveness.

"You're not a jerk, Jim. I appreciate your honesty. You have been a good friend. You know how I feel about you. I think we could have been good together, but I'm not going to be your "forever dating partner". I have a dream of falling in love with a man who is not afraid to love me back. It shouldn't have to be complicated or so difficult. It shouldn't be this painful or hard. You have been a good friend and you helped me realize that I can love again...I want to love again...and now I understand more clearly what it is I truly want for my life. I want it all...the whole package...love, marriage, and the happily ever after. You don't want the same things I want…and its okay."

Jim kissed her tenderly. "Gosh, he's a good kisser!" She thought. That is what seemed so confusing. The message he conveyed in his kisses was not the message of his heart. She made another mental addition to her list: Must enjoy kissing.

"We'll always be friends, though, right?" Jim asked trying to get her assurance.

Judy sighed, "Jim, I need some time. I don't think I want to see you for a while. You need some time, too. Go see your college student. You need to sort that one out. Do your dating thing. I'll be fine. Maybe, eventually, I'll date again too. I don't know…right now I need to focus on school and getting well."

"Are you going to be okay?" Jim asked with concern, stroking her hand tenderly.

"I'm fine…really. Don't worry about me. I will miss you even though you drive me nuts!" And they both hugged each other and laughed. "Take care, Jim…see you around!"

A kiss good-bye and it was over. Judy cried silently as she drove home and wondered, "Am I expecting too much? God, is there really someone out there for me?"

It was a strange having Jim out of her life. She had gotten used to calling him and talking to him about her day. Come to think of it…he really didn't call her that often. She usually called him. He always seemed glad to hear from her though. She decided she needed to add to her dream guy list, "He must call often".

She remembered how she and Jim hung out together like buddies. She sat with him at softball games and they went to movies, dances and dinners together. They would walk holding hands. People in Shilo were starting to think of them as a "couple" but Jim never acknowledged that. "Likes to hold hands…Must not be afraid to call me his girl friend," two more things added to the list.

"He is one strange guy…a nice guy…but strange!" Judy thought and felt confident in her decision to move on with her life

Judy's days were consumed with studying, working and sleeping. She had become accustomed to her disease and didn't anticipate the recovery as much as she used to.

"You have to leave it in God's hands." Judy's mother would tell her. And that is what she tried to do.

She had been sick for about a month now. "Surely it won't hang on much longer," She thought to herself.

Between classes Judy would check her cell phone for messages. "Hmmmm...Dad's trying to get a hold of me. I wonder what's up?" She decided to call back before her next class. "Dad? This is Judy. Is everything okay?"

"Oh! Judy! I'm so glad you called. It's your mother...she fell...she couldn't get her breath...they revived her, but she isn't doing well. You'd better come out right away!" Her father's voice was desperate.

"Is she conscious, Dad?" Judy asked

"Yes, yes, but she's on a ventilator to help her breath. It doesn't look good. You need to be here." He was crying now.

"Okay, okay, Dad. I'll come. I have to make arrangements here at school...but I'll come...don't worry. Tell Momma I'm on my way. Are the other's coming?" Judy's thoughts went to her siblings.

"We've contacted them...Shirley has helped me. I think they are coming...not sure about Rodney. Maybe you can try talking to him?" He asked hopefully.

"I'll try, Dad. But you know how he is...I don't know if he'll come and I'm not going to hang around until he decides. I am coming. I'll leave tonight. I'll call Rodney and let him know. He can decide for himself. It will be ok, Dad. Mom has been through tough times before...try not to worry."

"I'm glad you're coming...it will be better once everyone is here. She just looks so frail and small..." He couldn't go on.

"I'll see you tonight, Dad..."

"Will you be ok? Are you strong enough to make the drive?" Her father interrupted remembering that Judy is also sick.

"I'm sure Alicia and the kids will come with me. She can drive while I rest. It will be fine. I need to go now though so I can get things done. I'll see you later, Dad...I love you...tell Momma I love her too." And she hung up the phone and headed to her advisor's office.

She didn't notice the students around her exchanging greetings. They were unaware of the fear and sadness Judy felt deep inside.

"Sally? Can I come in?" Judy said as she knocked on the opened office door.

"Hey, Jude...c'mon in!" Sally said in her cheerful voice. She was working with her back turned to Judy at her desk. When she turned and saw Judy she said, "Oh my gosh! Are you ok? What's wrong, sweetie?" She could see the pain in Judy's face.

"It's my mom...my dad just called...she fell...she's on a ventilator...Sally, she could die...I need to go to her," Judy blurted out with tears welling up in her eyes.

"Are you going to be okay? Are you strong enough to make the trip alone? Do you have someone to help you drive?" She rattled through these questions so fast Judy didn't have a chance to answer them. Then she handed Judy her box of tissues.

"I'll be fine. Hopefully my daughter will drive with me...I have to call her," Judy said as she wiped her eyes and nose, "This is just so hard...I don't know how to prepare myself for this..."

"Just take it as it comes, Judy. Don't try to control it or manage it. You need to just get out there so you have a greater awareness of what you need to do to process it all. Don't worry about your classes. I'll let your other instructors know what is going on and you will have time to catch up when you get back. Are you okay to drive home?"

"Yes, thanks so much Sally. Please let my instructors know that I will get caught up and thank them for me for their understanding. I need to get home and get going...I think I may try and get a nap in before I go...or maybe I can sleep in the car while my daughter drives...oh, I also need to call work..." Judy didn't want to admit to how very tired she really was.

The drive to Harvey seemed extra long. Judy picked up her cell phone, "Alicia? This is Mom...Grandpa called and Grandma is in the hospital."

"Oh no! What happened?" Alicia asked with concern.

"She fell...she is on a ventilator to help her breath...it doesn't look good. I need to go out there but I am so tired I don't think I can make the drive myself. Can you drive it with me? Do you think they will give you the time off work?"

"Mom, this is important...I will go with you...they are just going to have to understand and deal with it. Don't worry about that; let's just get to Colorado to see Grandma. I'll meet you at home and notify the schools regarding the kids missing. It will be okay, mom...she'll be okay..." Alicia was trying hard to be convincing, but she knew her grandma was so weak and frail from her disease.

This time the trip to Colorado didn't allow for stops along the way for sight seeing or fun. Alex and Maggie Lu were exceptionally good on the drive. It was as if they knew the seriousness of the trip. They loved their Great Nana dearly.

"Will Great Nana be all right?" Maggie Lu asked from the back seat.

"We hope so, honey. We'll know more when we get there. We'll just keep her in our prayers, okay?" Judy reached back and caressed her granddaughter's leg.

"Are you okay, Alex?" He was sitting staring out the window.

"Yeah," he answered without looking away, "...just thinking."

"How about we play the "I Spy" game for a while?" Alicia said as she glanced at her children in the rear view mirror. It was time to lift the mood and created a distraction.

The kids loved to play that game; giving clues of some item they "spy" and the others trying to guess what it is. Maggie Lu almost always gave hints for the same item repeatedly or of the previous item from someone else, but everyone just played along with her and she would giggle and laugh. It was a game that their Great Nana often played with them and it was just the fun they needed.

"Darn! I forgot I was supposed to call Uncle Rod!" Judy rose up from the reclined car seat. "I better do that." And she got out her cell phone.

Rodney didn't answer his phone so Judy left him a brief message expressing that it was important he call their father or return her call regarding their mother in the hospital. She knew if she didn't mention the reason for her call he probably wouldn't bother calling back.

"Maybe if he knows Mom is in the hospital, he will actually call someone and talk to them." Judy said as she looked over at Alicia and put her phone away. "His life is just too busy and too important for the rest of us sometimes."

Rodney was a real estate broker in Florida. He detached from the family when the success of his career accelerated. Now, for what ever reason, he seemed to think he was better than everyone else and rarely made any family appearances. But he was Bonnie's baby boy and she would want him to know. Satisfied that she made the attempt, Judy laid back and surrendered to the sleep she so needed in order to function. The doctor had warned that stressful situations would increase her West Nile symptoms and she was starting to feel the effects of this stress on her body.

Arriving at her parent's apartment, Judy thought, "I didn't expect to be back here so soon." The air was crisp and cool as Judy and Alicia wearily started the process of unloading from the van. The kids had fallen asleep buckled in their seats. Bart and Sparky stood on the sidewalk and greeted them,

"I'm so glad you kids could come. How was the drive? How are you feeling, honey?" Bart said as he put his arm around his daughter.

"I'm okay, Daddy. Thank goodness Alicia was able to drive most of the way and I could rest…how's Momma?"

"Not too good, honey. She is really weak and so frustrated that she can't talk with that tube down her throat. The nurse said she is resting well tonight so we can go see her in the morning. She'll be so happy to see you though. Did you reach Rodney?"

"I tried, Dad…just got his voice mail. I left a message though for him to call you or someone. I told him Mom was in the hospital…so he knows that."

"Well, that's all we can do, I guess. I know she really wants to see him…she wants to see all of you, but you know how she is about him…he is her baby boy" There was the sound of disappointment in Bart's voice.

"I'm sure he'll call, Dad. He's just so busy with his work and life..." Judy stopped. Why did she do that? Why did she make up excuses for him? His behavior was inexcusable most of the time.

"Did Cheryl and David arrive?" Judy asked of her sister and husband from Washington.

"Yes, they arrived earlier today." Bart said as he carried the bags into the spare room. "They didn't bring any of the children with them though. It's too bad, because I know your mom loves to see those grandchildren and great-grand children when ever she can. They are staying at a motel close to the hospital."

"It will be good to see Cheryl again. I haven't seen her since...well, since my life changed." Judy said remembering back when to the family reunion on the lake.

It was the one time that Judy invited her family to come see how she was living with Dr. Dickhead on the lake. She wanted their approval so much, but knew it was going to be hard to get. Adultery was not something easily accepted, no matter the reason. No one ever thought Judy would do such a thing, but they agreed to meet her new companion and gather at the lake. It didn't go well.

Her sister's weren't impressed with the doctor's drinking and arrogant attitude. Her parents were politely tolerant. In fact, the only one that was impressed was Rodney, who stopped by briefly to see the family on his way to a convention in Omaha. The doctor and Rodney spent the day enjoying drinks, arguing politics and comparing stock market investments. Rodney barely spoke to any of the family.

The climax was when Roger (Dr. Dickhead) threw a drunken fit over having to pay for pizzas for the family. He had gone to town to pick them up and the family had gathered the money together to pay him when he brought them back. But he reacted before they had a chance to present the money to him. It was all of twenty-five dollars, and he landed in to Judy about her "worthless family" and how he "wasn't going to be stuck paying for everything!" Fortunately he stayed in the car while Judy gathered the pizzas and took them into the cabin.

Judy didn't think anyone noticed his rage, but Cheryl and David knew. Cheryl gave Judy the money from the family and Judy took it out to Roger in his car, threw it in his lap and said, "Here's your damn money. No one expects you to pay for anything. Why don't you go back to the bar you came from!"

It was the one time she stood up to him, probably because her family was all there and their presence gave her strength.

"Judy?" Her father's interrupted her thoughts and brought her back to the present, "Is there anything else you need tonight?"

"No...no...thanks, Dad. I'm just tired and need to sleep. We'll see you in the morning. Sleep well, Daddy." And she kissed him on the cheek.

"God Bless..." She heard him say softly as he entered his room.

"Why do all hospitals look and smell the same?" Alicia said to Judy as they rode the elevator the fifth floor and the Intensive Care Unit. At the family lounge area they met up with the rest of the family.

"Judy!" It's so good to see you again! How are you feeling? We heard you have West Nile. That has to be so frightening. It hasn't reached our state yet, but it is sure strong here in Colorado, too." Cheryl reached out her arms to hug her sister.

Cheryl was tall with beautiful red hair and green eyes. Her skin was light, like porcelain with just a few freckles across her nose and cheeks. She had a simple beauty about her that radiated from the inside outward.

"Hi, Judy!" David said as he approached his wife and sister-in-law. "You look good...but thinner than you were."

"Yeah, the one advantage of this illness is weight loss. I've lost about twenty-five pounds...I'm just not hungry and I've lost my sense of taste. The doctors say it should be temporary and will return when Virus leaves my system." Judy didn't realize the weight loss was that noticeable. "I'm adjusting to it though. I just get really, really tired. It's a very strange illness."

"You always did do things a little strange." Judy heard a familiar voice from just outside the door. Then Rodney entered the room.

"Rod! You must have gotten my message!" Judy looked surprised.

"Yes, I took the Red Eye flight here. Thanks for letting me know." His eyes filled with tears and he continued, "She looks so small and frail, Jude...I don't think I can do this!" And he fell into her arms.

Judy and Rodney had always had a special relationship growing up. She was the youngest daughter and he the baby boy. When Rodney was just ten years old, their mother had been very ill and Judy took care of Rodney. She was in high school and took him everywhere with her and when he misbehaved she disciplined him. She was like his temporary mother.

"It will be okay, Rod. You need to be here and you need to do it for her. It isn't easy for any of us, but we'll do it for her...for Daddy," Judy spoke firmly as she looked into her brother's eyes.

"I...I...just don't know if I can..." Rodney said softly.

"You will!" Judy responded firmly, "You can't bury yourself in business this time. You have to face this and be here!"

"Who wants to go next?" Shirley asked as she entered the room dabbing at her eyes. "Judy, I'm glad you and Alicia are here. "Hi, kiddos!" she said as she hugged Alex and Maggie Lu.

"Great Nana is very sick," Maggie Lu said, her eyes big and watery, "Can I see her? Can I see Great Nana?" Her lip quivered as she spoke. She had a very special relationship with her Great Nana. Maggie Lu had asthma and knew what it was like to be short of breath and needing a machine to help you breath sometimes. She had a nebulizer that she used occasionally.

Shirley looked up at Alicia and Judy for assistance with the answer but they were uncertain what to say. "Let's wait just a little bit, okay? I think Great Nana would really like for you to make her a pretty picture. I knew you and Alex were coming and so I brought some paper and crayons for you to make her something really special. Do you think you guys could work on that for a while so that Mommy and Grandma can visit Great Nana for a little bit?"

Shirley was incredible with kids even though she and Terry chose not to have any of their own. Kids just seemed to gravitate to her.

Cheryl and Judy often said it was because she was so short and they felt she was one of them.

Shirley resembled their mother in stature and appearance. They both had dark hair and beautiful blue eyes. Now their mother's hair was salt and pepper gray, but Shirley still managed to keep hers dark…with the help of Clairol.

When their mother was healthier they could exchange clothing, but not anymore. Bonnie had lost a great amount of weight and was almost skeletal in appearance and Shirley had gained weight as she got older and worked hard to keep it from becoming a problem. The three sisters were so different, but shared so much.

"How many can go see her at one time?" Alicia asked, hoping that she could go with her mother.

"They only want two or three at a time." Shirley answered. "Daddy's in there with her now, but I'm going to try and get him to leave for a little bit and get some lunch. He just doesn't want to leave her side." She blinked back her tears.

"We'll go back and let Dad know that you want him to come out and get something to eat, okay?" Judy gently placed her hand on Shirley's shoulder.

Shirley nodded, "That would be great, thanks, Jude."

Bonnie's tiny, frail body was surrounded by pillows and nestled in the hospital bed. Sitting by her side was her devoted and loving life partner and friend. She appeared to be sleeping and he was just staring blankly at the rail on the bed. It was as if he was reflecting on scenes from their long life together. The sound of the respirator was pumping and hissing, providing the life saving oxygen into her lungs, together with the beep of the monitor they rhythmically filled the cubicle, which was Bonnie's space of care.

"Dad?" Judy whispered so not to alarm her sweet father from his trance.

Bart turned to the voice beside him. There were tears in his eyes as he looked up to Judy, "Oh Judy, I'm so glad you are here…look, Mother, its Judy and Alicia, too. They've come to see you." And he released her hand and placed it on Judy's.

"Hi Momma...I hear you took a tumble?" Judy said fighting back the tears as she noticed the bruising on the right side of her mother's face. Bonnie's eyes lit up when she saw Judy. She seemed to want to say something, but the ventilator prohibited her from being able to speak.

"Its okay, Momma. Don't try to talk. Just relax. Alicia and I are going to sit with you while Daddy goes with Shirley and the rest to get some lunch." Judy turned to her father, "Its okay, Daddy, you need to get something to eat. We'll be here, now go...its okay."

Bart looked at his wife who gave him an approving nod and then he bent down and gently kissed her on the forehead. "I'll be right back, Babe." He said to her lovingly. Her eyes smiled up at his.

Bonnie turned her focus toward Judy. There was a sense of determination in the way she squeezed her hand and the look in her eyes. She was so frustrated because she couldn't speak. She released the hold on Judy's hand and weakly made an effort to try and write a message on Judy's chest. She was trying to form letters with her lips, the merciless tube of the ventilator preventing the formations.

Her lips would draw into an "O" shape; while her hand struggled to write letters on Judy's shirt. "It looks like an "F"...I think that's the letter..." Alicia said and Bonnie tried to express her agreement.

The monitors were reacting to Bonnie's exertion and soon a nurse came into the room. "It's very important to keep her calm. I know it is frustrating for you because she can't talk, but she must not get overly excited. Please don't try and get her to write or talk."

Bonnie dropped her hand in exhaustion. She rocked her head from side to side and the frustration was so obvious in her eyes.

Judy bent over her mother stroking her head saying, "Momma, let's do what the nurse says, okay? Just relax. When you're better, you can tell us all about what you were trying to say. I just want to sit and hold your hand for now, okay?"

Bonnie seemed to calm down as a single tear gently rolled from her right eye, across her temple and to the pillow propped under her head. She seemed to rest comfortably as Alicia and Judy told her about the dive out with the kids and how they had played "I Spy" for hours.

Judy stepped away allowing Alicia time to hold her grandma's hand. Alicia struggled to keep from crying. Her grandma had always been there for her. She always knew just what to do to help in difficult situations. How she wished she could return the favor now. Alicia had to turn her face away and let the tears flow. Judy wiped her daughter's eyes and stood with her arm over her shoulder. Bonnie was sleeping now as the rhythm of the machines continued their eerie lullaby.

"They're moving Momma to another room and they're removing the tube," Shirley said blankly. Her eyes were red from crying.

"Mom has requested the tube to be removed. She wants to try to breath on her own. She wants to be able to talk to her family. It's her decision." Shirley had been in the room with Mom and Dad for some time.

The doctors explained the possible risks and consequences involved with taking Bonnie off the ventilator. But Bonnie felt she could do it if they would just let her try. So they agreed to give her the chance and she decided to refuse having it replaced.

"What will happen?" Cheryl asked as she looked up from her magazine.

"She will either start breathing on her own, or she won't," Shirley explained.

"What do you mean...she won't...you mean...no...she can't...she must..." Cheryl was rambling from the emotion behind the decision her mother was making. David put his arm around Cheryl as she started to cry.

"Listen, this is really hard...especially on Dad. He doesn't want to lose her, but she doesn't want to live this way. We need to honor her decision whether we agree with it or not. There is no easy way to deal with this. We need to spend some time with her, but carefully. We don't want to wear her out." Shirley was determined to carry out her mother's wishes. Everyone was quiet in thought.

Judy and Alicia went to Bonnie's room.

"Hey, Mom..." Judy said as she approached the bed. "How are you?" Bonnie looked up at her daughter and smiled. Her eyes seemed bluer than they have ever been and she was calm and quite.

"I...I'm...fine...h-honey." Her voice was raspy and hoarse from the irritation of the ventilator tube. "How are you f-f-feeling?" She was concerned about Judy's condition.

"Oh Mom, I'm ok...don't worry about me. I'm just so glad you are doing better." And Judy watched her mother take a long slow breath. It was obvious she was still struggling to breath.

Alicia stepped up to the bed. "Hi Grandma, its Alicia...Brad couldn't come because Jen is due any day now. They send their love though."

"How is J-Jen f-f-feeling?" Bonnie asked.

"She's doing fine, Mom," Judy replied, "They are so anxious for this baby. I've never seen them so happy. Matthew and Jasmine are excited, too."

"A new b-b-baby...h-h-how wonderful...l-l-life goes on," Bonnie whispered.

"Mom, what were you trying to tell us before when you couldn't speak?"

Bonnie smiled and breathed deeply and thoughtfully. She held Judy's hand and with a gentle voice said, "I was trying to tell you to have FAITH," and then she took Alicia's hand and said, "HOPE...I was trying to say hope...have hope. I was so f-f-frustrated..."

"You should rest now, Mom. We'll take your advice and cling to our faith and hold on to our hope. You always said that faith and hope are the wings we soar with..." Judy squeezed her mother's hand gently.

"It's true, you know...I love you...I love you both," and Bonnie closed her eyes to sleep. Alicia kissed her grandma's hand.

The rest of Bart and Bonnie's grandchildren started arriving. The apartment community where Bart and Bonnie lived had a club house that provided a good gathering place for the families. Bonnie was holding on, but the doctors knew it was just a matter of time before her ability to breath on her own would be gone. She wanted the family around her and she wanted to be able to talk and laugh with them as much as possible.

Cheryl and David's youngest daughter Tessa arrived from college in Seattle. As she stood at the foot of her grandma's bed,

Bonnie said, "Tess, you are so beautiful standing there. You look like an angel." Tessa was wearing a white sweater and jeans and standing next to her sister, Jean and brother-in-law, Clark.

Alex, Maggie Lu, Marty and Meagan (Cheryl and David's grandchildren) all gathered around their Great Nana's bed and played "I Spy" as Bonnie watched, listened and smiled; occasionally her hand would gently reach out to touch them and they would smiled back at her. Suddenly the phone in the room rang and Judy answered.

"Hey, Mom…we're at the hospital!" It was Brad. Jen had gone into labor.

"Just a minute…I'm going to let you tell Grandma." And Judy held the phone to her mother's ear.

"H-h-hello?" Bonnie said weakly

"Hi Grandma! It's Brad. We wanted to let you know that a new great-grand baby is coming real soon. We just got to the hospital. It won't be long now." Brad was excited.

"No…it won't be l-l-long now," Bonnie responded, knowing it applied to her time as well, "I am s-s-so h-h-happy for you. F-f-faith and h-h-hope are the wings we soar with…" she said to encourage her grandson.

Brad was fighting back the tears on the other end of the line. "I love you Grandma. You were always there for me. I just wish I could be there for you, now. We both…we all…love you so very much!" In the hospital room, 500 miles away, Jen gently held her husband's hand as the tears rolled down his cheeks.

Bonnie felt the love burn warmly in her heart. "I know…I know, honey…and I l-l-l-love you, too. God b-b-bless." A tear fell from Bonnie's eye.

Judy spoke into the receiver, "We're praying for you here, Son. Let Jen know that too. Call as soon as you know."

"We will, Mom…it won't be for a little while yet. I love you, Mom…sorry I'm not there with you…"

"Don't even think about that…you're having a baby! Enjoy the moment…I wish I could be there with you, too. But you know we're all connected anyway. Call us as soon as the baby is here. We'll be waiting."

"We will...tell everyone hello from us. Bye Mom."
Bye...oh...and God bless!"
Bonnie smiled up at her daughter and said, "Thank you." She was getting tired but she motioned for Judy to come close. Judy lowered her ear to her mother's lips.

"Judy..." Bonnie whispered softly, "I will tell Miranda h-h-hello from you w-w-when I g-g-get there..."

Judy kissed her mother gently as tears filled her eyes, "Tell her I'm sorry, too...thank you, Momma."

Love poured from Bonnie's eyes as she gazed at her family all gathered there around the room. "God bless." She whispered.

It was getting late and the nurses said it would be good for Bonnie to get some rest. "It's amazing!" They told the family outside of the room, "She is doing so well. We didn't expect her to hold on this long. She seems to be resting comfortably. Why don't you all go and get some rest. We'll call you if there is any change otherwise we will see you all tomorrow."

Bart slipped back into the room. Judy stood in the doorway and watched as her father leaned over the bed gently stroking his wife's head.

"You are so beautiful!" He said to her looking lovingly into her eyes and clutching her small hand in his. She was beautiful although her outer shell was deteriorating her inner beauty radiated from her.

Bonnie looked into the eyes of the love of her life and whispered, "I love you."

It was the most beautiful moment Judy ever experienced and one she would never forget. As she silently observed her parents exchange of love, she realized what they have between them is all she has ever wanted and she prayed, "God, please help me find a love like this...please." Then she took her father's arm and they left the room together but Bart turned and blew a kiss to his beloved wife; she knowingly smiled back.

The families all decided to gather at Bart and Bonnie's apartment club house and visit before retiring for the evening. They were convinced that Bonnie was going to surprise them all and pull through again as she had done so many times before. She was a fighter with an incredible zest for life.

What they didn't know was that Bonnie was tired and ready to go home. Not back to her apartment with Bart, but home to the place that she knew was prepared for her. She was going to the place where her mother and father, sister and brother were all waiting...and her beautiful granddaughter, Miranda. They had gone there some time before her and it was time for her to meet them.

The phone call came around two o'clock in the morning. "Mr. Williams...this is the nurse at Faith Lutheran Hospital. You need to come as soon as possible. Your wife is asking for you..."

Bart interrupted, "We'll be there right away!"

The drive to the hospital seemed longer than usual although there was no traffic on the roads. Shirley and Terry were bringing Dad. Cheryl, David and Rodney were on their way. Judy and Alicia drove their van. Tess, stayed with the great-grandkids at the hotel.

The night was calm and cool and the moon was shining brightly, seeming to lead the way to the hospital. There was road construction along the way, but Judy drove right through it without delay as if guided by some unknown force.

As Judy turned the corner toward the hospital Alicia suddenly looked at her mother and said, "She's gone. I can feel it. She's gone, Mom."

Judy looked at her daughter with tears in her eyes and said, "No she's not...she can't be...she guided us here through all that road work. No...you must be wrong!"

But Alicia knew she wasn't.

As they exited the elevator on the fifth floor the nurses were waiting for them. "She's gone...I'm so sorry. It was just a few minutes ago...it was very peaceful for her..."

"No! No! Not yet...oh, God, please...not yet..." and Judy entered her room. There her mother lay in all her peaceful beauty. Overcome with grief, Judy reached for her mother and lifted her into her arms. Her body was still so warm. Death was still so fresh.

She held the small, frail shell of her mother in her arms and rocked her gently sobbing, "Oh, Momma, Momma…I'm so sorry I wasn't here…I'm so sorry…I don't want you to go…oh, God…oh, God…"

Alicia touched her mother's shoulder sobbing and sharing her grief. Judy gently laid her mother back on the pillow and smoothed her soft hair. Bonnie looked so peaceful…and then Judy's cell phone rang.

"Mom? We have a little girl!" It was Brad. Jen had given birth. "She's beautiful, Mom. We're going to name her Faith Hope Braxtin. I can't wait for you to see her…Mom?"

"Oh, Brad…I'm so happy for you. She sounds perfect…the name is perfect. Is Jen okay?" Judy asked, tearfully, and then added, "What time was she born?"

"Just a few minutes ago, Mom. It was great. I cut the cord. I swear she looked at me and smiled, Mom. It was so amazing!"

Judy smiled at the possibility of the souls of her mother and new granddaughter passing each other in route to their destinations of heaven and earth.

"Brad, this is such good news…but I have some sad news I need to share with you. Grandma died just a few minutes ago…she went peacefully. She was ready to go home." Judy could hear her son sobbing. "It's ok, Brad. We have a new life. It's wonderful. Grandma is dancing in heaven!"

"I'm so sorry, Mom…how's Grandpa?" Brad asked.

"He isn't here yet, but will be soon. You take care. Give Jen a big hug from me and kiss that new granddaughter…little Faith Hope. Can't wait to see her, but it may be a while now. We need to make the funeral arrangements. I'll let you know. I love you…and God bless."

Bart stepped into the room and saw his sweetheart lying so still on the bed. Dropping to his knees next to her he wept as his children gathered around them in a loving good bye.

Rodney was having a hard time processing his mother's death. He informed the family that he wouldn't be staying to help with the funeral arrangements. There had been a "business emergency" and he had to leave. He justified his actions saying, "You know Mom…she always said she didn't want a lot of attention when she died. She would understand." There was no convincing him otherwise…and then…he was gone.

Shirley and Cheryl worked with the funeral home to get things arranged for Bonnie's cremation and memorial service in Colorado. It was determined that there would be another memorial service in the spring when Bonnie's ashes would be buried at her family's cemetery plot in Briarwood, Nebraska. Judy would take the ashes back with her and keep them at her home until spring. Judy's job was to help her father go through papers and some of her mother's things.

The service at the funeral home chapel was small and very private. Family members were able to say their goodbyes to Bonnie as she lay peacefully in the simple coffin at the front of the chapel. Judy had prepared her mother's hair and make-up for viewing. She knew her mother wouldn't want to be overly made up by someone who didn't even know how she liked to wear her hair. The time Judy spent with her mother was what she needed to give her closure. She could sense her mother's spirit in the room with her as she prepared the body for viewing. Others might think it strange, but Judy didn't care. This was her Momma and she was saying goodbye.

After the service Bonnie's body would be cremated and the ashes put in a container of the family's choosing. Maggie Lu helped Judy pick out a "special jar" to keep the ashes in. She chose a blue one with big sunflowers on it because she knew Great Nana liked blue and those kinds of flowers.

There was a luncheon at the club house. Bonnie's clown collection pieces were used on the tables for centerpieces. The grand children and great-grand children made up memory boards displaying Bonnie's life in pictures. The last clown outfit that Bonnie made, which she never did get to wear, was on display as well. Many of the relatives came from all around to offer their condolences.

Shirley worked on getting the apartment organized for Bart and promised him she would stop by often to help him out with things. Sparky sat patiently by the door waiting for Bonnie to come home.

They were all a little concerned about their father's ability to stay alone in the apartment, but decided to let him try it for a while. He was starting to develop signs of confusion.

Cheryl, David and Tessa went back to Washington. Judy, Alicia, Alex and Maggie Lu drove back to Nebraska with Bonnie's ashes in the blue sunflower jar.

Chapter 7
Getting the Ducks in a Row

"Well, Momma…this is going to be your home for a while," Judy spoke to the blue jar with big bright sunflowers as she placed it on the cherry wood shelf in her living room, "I suppose some people might think this strange…having your mother's remains sitting on a shelf in the living room, but I don't care. It's only temporary, until we have your burial in the spring." She put her mother's picture next to the jar.

It was the picture she had taken when they were in the backyard of Shirley's house. Bonnie had leaned on the porch railing, resting her head on her hand and smiled that beautiful smile. It was spontaneous and beautiful. And Judy loved it. "How strange it will be not calling and talking to you," Judy said to the picture as if it could hear her, "I sure miss you." Then the phone rang.

"Hey, kiddo!" It was Jessica. "Just a reminder about the hayrack ride this weekend. You are still coming?"

Jessica and Ted had a hayrack ride and potluck every year. It was a lot of fun. Judy had gone with Dr. Dickhead once and then alone once, because he refused to go. This year she was going with Jim. They just decided since they were both going anyway, they might as well go together.

"Yeah, I plan on it…I don't know how much fun I'll be…I'm still not feeling that well, but I'm going. Actually, Jim and I are planning on going together."

"Really?" Jessica sounded pleased, but surprised, "I thought you guys decided to quit seeing each other.'

"We did. It's just a friend thing...nothing more. We just figured since we are both going we would just go together...it's no big deal." Judy was trying to convince herself as well as Jessica.'

"Uh-huh...yeah...right," Jessica laughed as she replied, "You guys need to figure it out!"

"Hey, I know what I want and it isn't Jim. He isn't meeting my list," Judy said in defense.

"List? What list?" Jessica was curious now, "You mean to tell me you've created a list? What...like some sort of standard for a guy to meet, or what?"

"Well, sort of...I just don't seem to do well at this dating thing...and look at my past choices in men! I decided I needed to set some standards...sort of a guide for me, mostly. It's a kind of reminder for me of what I really want...what I know I need...and what I hope for." Judy pulled her list from her purse. She kept it with her to refer to and reflect on.

"What do you have on this list?" Jessica just had to know. She had never imagined such a thing. But then how could she. She married her high school sweetheart; a man who was gentle and kind and a good provider and partner. They had the most amazing relationship and Judy envied Jessica for it.

"I'm not going to share everything with you, but I'll give you some highlights from the list. "You see, I have a list of *Necessary Characteristics* and a list *of Preferred Characteristics...*" she said as she glanced down her list determining what she wanted to share with her friend.

"I don't believe this, girl! You amaze me!" Jessica chirped.

"Okay...here goes...for *Necessary* he has to be honest and trustworthy...have a sense of faith, but not overly religious...more like confident in what he believes. He has to be emotionally mature and secure and polite and considerate...respectful of all people and things. He must have wisdom, which I feel is far more important than intelligence and most important of all he must not be afraid of commitment…he has to believe in marriage…I won't be someone's forever girlfriend!" It was just a portion of the list.

"Those aren't unreasonable…it's a good list," Jessica said, "What are some of the *Preferred* things?" Jessica was amazed at her friend's determination and faith to find that "one good guy".

Judy continued, "I'd like it if he was tall…at least taller than five foot-nine inches"…and somewhere between the ages of forty-five to sixty…a non-smoker…non-drinker, at least not an alcoholic…romantic, knows what makes a woman feel special…flexible, able to give and take easily…willing to learn new things…good understanding of family…and a strong leader, but willing follower." She carefully folded the list and put it back in her purse. "What do you think?"

"Wow! I hope you find him. You deserve it…you've definitely had your share of losers!" Jessica said jokingly.

"You know, Jess…I think I will. Somewhere out there is a guy looking for a girl like me. Somehow we'll find each other. In the meantime, I will be at the hayrack ride with my *friend* Jim," as she laughed.

"Okay, then…we'll see you this weekend…make sure to add *likes to have fun* to your list and we'll get along fine! Bye girlfriend!" Judy hung up the phone and thought about her list.

"He's out there," She said to herself, "I just know it."

The hayrack ride was a blur. Judy was so tired and the symptoms from her illness were very strong. She wrapped herself in a blanket and slept most of the time. Jim didn't talk to her much. He wasn't rude. Jim couldn't be rude. He was just distant and tired of her being so tired all of the time. He spent most of the evening talking to his Shilo friends. Judy finally convinced him to take her home. It just wasn't any fun anymore and she was too tired and sick to care. She was starting her second month of illness.

* * *

"The turkey smells great, Alicia!" Judy said as she peeked at the golden bird in the oven. "I'm so glad we could have Thanksgiving dinner at your new house. You've done an incredible job decorating. I just love the loft. I'd have my studio up there if I lived here, you know."

"I know Mom. That's my office where I do my homework." Alicia had returned to college to work on her teaching degree. Judy was so glad she went back to college. Having her cosmetology license was good, but she knew Alicia was capable of so much more. She was a very talented and creative person.

"You should write a book, Alicia," Judy told her daughter, "You have such a wonderful imagination and way with words. I love to read your stories."

"Yeah, maybe in my next life, Mom," Alicia responded as she started the blender to whip the potatoes.

"Hey Leesh…" Brad called out from the other room. "Are we having your special potatoes?"

Brad loved the way his sister mashed the potatoes with the skins still on; adding garlic powder, pepper, real butter and sour cream. "They are so awesome!" he added as he and Jen sat in the living room admiring their little daughter, Faith Hope.

"She is so beautiful!" Brad said as he sat with his arm around Jen, "We are so lucky!"

"We are so blessed!" Jen replied with a smile. Their lives had changed dramatically since the birth of their daughter, but they were happier than they had ever been.

Jasmine peered over her mother's arm at the new baby sister before her and paused briefly from sucking her thumb to smile and gently touch the baby's hand. "My baby!" she said proudly.

"I get the wishing bone!" Matthew called out running past Judy as she lifted the turkey from the oven.

It was always a contest among the grandchildren to be the first to claim the wish bone in the turkey. This year, Matthew is the victor.

"You are quick, Matthew! Good job, but remember, you have to let it dry out good and long in order for it to work right," Judy reminded him as she placed the golden bird on her grandmother's platter.

That was also a long standing tradition; to use the old china platter with its flower accents and gold rim. Judy remembered the same platter being used at Thanksgiving dinner when she was growing up and the vision of that memory danced in her head.

"Mom, you want to say the prayer?" Alicia asked as the family all joined hands around the table. "Thanks, honey...I'd be happy to." And they bowed their heads as the little ones peeked to see what was going on around them.

"Dear God, we thank you for this food which you have provided for us as nourishment to our bodies. Bless our families, God...those with us, those away, and those with you. Keep us mindful of our purpose here on Earth and help us to serve you as you have planned for us. We thank you for our many blessings." And everyone said, "Amen."

It was a tradition on Thanksgiving for each person to share something they were thankful for. Judy was certain the rest of her family was doing the same where ever they were. Dad would be at Shirley and Terry's in Colorado, Cheryl and David would have the family gathered at their home in Washington, and Rodney was no doubt visiting some tropical island somewhere. He didn't do holidays.

And so they began...Alicia was thankful that no one was hurt in the fire and that she had insurance to replace what was lost. Alex was thankful for his mom, his dad, his dog Daisy and sister "Mag-pie". Maggie Lu was thankful that they were going to Disney World and that Great Nana is in heaven with Aunt Miranda. Matthew was thankful he got the wish bone. Jasmine just said "Thank you" and smiled. Jen was thankful for her family and for the fairly easy birth of their new daughter. Brad looked at his mother and said, "Thank God you are here!" And Judy was thankful for them all and for God's grace and protection.

* * *

The first semester of college was winding down and finals were just around the corner. Things were becoming stressful for Judy as she juggled work, school, health and family. Things in the lab were going well, though. The weather was colder now so the sweltering heat inside the lab was no longer a problem. The cloning of an Anthole Begonia, which had never been done before, thrilled her. There were thousands of them developing in the lab and hundreds had already been transferred to the greenhouses.

The West Nile symptoms were still prevalent and she had just accepted the fact that she might feel this way for the rest of her life. The fatigue created an emptiness inside her…a darkness that she was trying to live with. She missed that light she used to have and the energy and warm glow it gave her. Her greatest sense of achievement was her education as she had maintained a 3.8 grade point average even with the difficulties she faced during that first semester. How she loved her business classes, especially the communication classes and marketing, but the accounting and business math were a struggle; though she passed them with a B and B+.

The knock on the door was unexpected. Judy didn't receive a lot of visitors. Occasionally Mr. Klassen, the land lord, would stop by to check on the heat tape he had on the pipes in the cellar to keep them from freezing; otherwise it was Alicia or one of the grandchildren.

Judy and Dottie usually spent most evenings alone; Dottie snoozing on Judy's lap and Judy studying with KPGY playing her favorite country music in the background. Sometimes she watched T.V., but not that often. It was too hard to follow a program and study at the same time.

As she approached the door she recognized the figure standing there behind the glass.

"Hi Judy…Merry Christmas." It was Jim…she hadn't heard from him in weeks…since the hay rack ride. "I was thinking of you and thought you'd like a little Christmas cheer." He was holding a basket wrapped in colored cellophane and filled with an assortment of fruit and nuts."

"Hello, Jim…thank you…that is sweet…come in out of the cold." Judy took the basket and set it on the table. "How are things in Shilo? Are you ready for Christmas?"

"It's been busy…you know how it is this time of year for mail carriers!" He said with a laugh.

"Oh, I suppose it would be busier than normal." Judy continued the conversation politely.

"How are you doing? How have you been feeling?" Jim asked as he looked around the room.

"I'm doing okay. Just trying to get through the finals at school…what a killer! I've adjusted to being sick…its better…I guess. Do you want to sit down?" He seemed to want to stay.

"Sure, I can stay for a while…unless you need to study…you look good, Judy," Jim said as he removed his coat and sat down on the futon sofa.

"I need a break from studying anyway. How are you? How are your daughters?" Judy was trying to keep the conversation going, but really had nothing much to say to him.

"They are good. Looking forward to winter break from school…and Christmas, of course," Jim responded. And they sat down…not knowing what to say. It was awkward for them both.

Jim turned to Judy and said, "I've missed you. I've been thinking about you…about us…do you think…maybe we could go out again sometime?"

Judy couldn't believe what she was hearing…"Not again!" She thought to herself and she took a deep breath. "Jim, you're a nice guy, but no I don't think I want to go out with you right now. I'm just not into dating right now. I have my goals set for school and I barely have enough energy to manage that, work, and recovering. I just don't think it is a good idea right now." She was trying to be nice, but firm.

The idea of having someone to go to movies with again or out to eat with was tempting, but after observing her parents in their last moments together, she realized that she wanted something more. And she believed it was out there for her…somewhere.

Jim stood and put on his jacket. "I understand. You sound very confident and determined in your plans for school. I'm happy for you."

"Jim, maybe someday I'll feel like dating again...I don't know. It's just that after seeing my mom and dad together and the love they have for each other, I realize that I want that even stronger now. Maybe there is a guy out there who feels the same way. I just hope I have the energy to deal with it if I meet him. For now, I am just working on getting the things done I need to accomplish and getting my ducks in a row...you know what I mean?" She walked Jim to the door.

"Sure...I understand...I'm happy for you. Can I still call you sometime...just to talk?" Jim asked as he went out the door.

"Okay...yeah...that's fine, Jim. You take care now and tell your daughters *Merry Christmas* from me...and thanks again for the fruit basket...that was nice of you."

She waved good-bye and closed the door. "Oh, brother!" she said as she leaned on the door. "Dottie, that is one confused guy!" she said to the little dog looking up at her and tilting her head.

"A fruit basket? You'd think if he was trying to get me to go out with him again he'd have brought flowers or something..." she said as she put the fruit in the refrigerator...but flowers would be too intimate and she didn't want them from him anyway.

"Grandma I get to put the star on the tree!" Maggie Lu said excitedly, running up the walk to Judy.

"Watch your step Lu Lu! There might be ice!" Judy warned her grand daughter, meeting her at the steps outside her front door. "What time is the program tonight?" she asked Alicia who was walking up with Alex.

"Not until seven, but the kids have to be there early. Do you want to ride with us or drive yourself?" Alicia stomped the snow off her boots before entering the house, "Oh, it feels good in here...nice and warm. It smells good too!"

Judy was cooking a roast in the oven with carrots and potatoes, just like her mom used to make. "Thanks, I wanted us to have something good to eat before we go. I'm sure they will have cookies at the church following the program. So you get to put the star on the tree!" Judy helped Maggie Lu with her coat and scarf.

"Yep, and Alex has to say a special part, too. It will be so fun!" Maggie Lu was excited about everything this time of year.

"Merry Christmas to all and God Bless..." It was the closing line of the children's program and Clarmar Presbyterian Church.

"We're so glad you came tonight. I hope you and your daughter will come to service on Sunday," the pastor said, greeting Judy as she approached the exit.

"Thank you Pastor...we'll certainly try. I enjoyed it very much." Although Judy knew what and who she believed in, she hadn't been a regular church attendee for some time.

In the past she put too much faith in people and not enough in God. She learned the hard way that even good and godly people are still human and because of that they can do things that hurt you. She had confided in a pastor once and he betrayed her confidence. She was suspicious of most pastors now and preferred to study the Bible on her own, occasionally watching a church service on T.V. She did miss the fellowship she experienced as part of a church body though.

"Maybe this little church wouldn't be so bad," she thought to herself as she looked around, "but what would they think of me if they knew how I left my husband for another man...this is a small town...I don't know...I think I'll just play it safe for a while."

"Mom?" Alicia asked seeing Judy was deep in thought, "Are you coming downstairs for cookies?"

"No, you all go ahead. I'm feeling kind of tired tonight and think I'm going to go home to bed. Alex, Maggie Lu you did a really good job. I am so proud of you. Go and enjoy your cookies! I'll talk to you tomorrow," Judy blew kisses and the kids pretended to catch them; placing them on their lips and giggling.

"Good night Grandma!" They said as they hurried down the stairs to the basement.

"Are you okay, Mom?" Alicia could sense something in her mother's eyes.

"I'm fine, honey…just tired. I'll talk to you tomorrow, good night…"

"Goodnight, Mom…get a good rest. It's Christmas Eve tomorrow!" Alicia had that sound of excitement in her voice she used to get as a little girl.

Tradition was that gifts were opened on Christmas Eve in the Braxtin house. That tradition still carried over. They also had breaded shrimp and French fries for supper and no gifts could be opened until the food was eaten and the dishes done. Judy remembered how Lenny used to antagonize the kids by eating real slow. He loved to tease them. They loved their father even though he was sometimes so hard on them.

Christmas Eve also worked well for Brad and Alicia to celebrate with their mother because they all went to their father's house on Christmas Day. Lenny had remarried and his new wife was good to the kids and grandkids. Judy was thankful for that but often wondered what her life with Lenny was like. Was she able to make him happy? Was he good to her? Judy hoped so. She never hated Lenny even though he was hurtful and felt so badly about what she had done to him…to their marriage. She really wanted him to find happiness. It was good to have her children and grandchildren around her again for the holiday.

Shirley had called a few weeks ago and said she was really concerned about Dad. He was getting very forgetful and fell a couple of times. They were going to have him move in with them for a while and see how it goes. She told Judy, "We have the guest room with its own bath and we could fix it up like a little apartment for him. I just don't feel right having him at the apartment alone. Sparky is getting really old and is having health problems. I'm afraid we're going to have to put him down soon and then Daddy would be all alone. This will be better." Judy was in complete agreement. Cheryl and David agreed also. A message was left with Rodney who was away on business again.

Gone were the days of huge family Christmas gatherings. What fun they were when Judy was small! Uncle Ed used to dress up like Santa and pass out gifts. All the aunts and uncles and cousins were there, packed into the tiny farm house in Briarwood. As Judy looked around the room at her children and grandchildren she was thankful for what she had. On the cherry wood shelf in the corner of the room sat the bright blue jar with big yellow sunflowers and the picture of Bonnie smiling approvingly. Toward the top of the Christmas tree was a little brass angel blowing a kiss and engraved with the name, Miranda Lynn Braxtin…the holidays were forever a painful memory of those no longer present.

2003 was coming to an end. It was a difficult year for Judy Braxtin and her family and one with many growing pains. Having successfully completed her first semester of college, Judy was beginning to see her life take shape again. She always thought she was smart, but had been put down and kept down so long that she lost faith in what she was really capable of. To her amazement she made the Dean's Honor list and received recognition in the mail and in the local newspaper. Her classes were set for the second semester and she was feeling more confident and alive than ever before. And then it happened…one morning…she woke up and it was gone! That empty, dark feeling had lifted! The light was back on and she felt wonderful! As quickly as the West Nile Virus had entered her body it left just as suddenly. Although her immune system was weakened, she started feeling like her old self again and was ready to take on the world!

Chapter 8
A New Year - New Adventures

It was New Years Eve 2003. Judy was in the lab working on her Begonias when Jane, a DJ on KPGY was encouraging people to call in a request for a song and tell their New Year's Resolution. Normally Judy didn't use her cell phone while working, but she decided to do it this time.

The voice on the other end of the line was familiar to Judy because she listened to her often, "KPGY, this is Jane do you have a request and resolution to share?"

Judy hesitated but then spoke up, "Yes, yes I do. Could you please play *I Want to Do It All* by Terri Clark? It is my theme song for 2004. My resolution is to have a new adventure every month for a year." There, she said it. Somehow speaking it made it more real and definite

"Wow! Really? That sounds pretty cool! What type of adventures are you planning?" She got the attention of Jane, the DJ.

"Well, my first adventure to start out the year is to go to the New Year's Eve Rodeo Ball at Melrose tonight." Judy didn't expect to be asked to define her adventures.

"Hey! We'll be there!" Jane replied with enthusiasm.

KPGY was the main sponsor of the event which was held every New Years Eve in Melrose. The celebration starts with an indoor

Rodeo (with bull riders and everything) and then a dance afterward with a band. Although Judy had never gone to the event before, she listened to the advertisement about it on KPGY and decided it sounded like fun. She was trying to step out of her safety zone and try and meet people. Most people had dates for the event...Judy was going alone. She decided seeing a rodeo would be entertaining and checking out the cowboys might be fun, too; although she had no intention of meeting anyone there.

"So, let me get this straight..." Jane was really curious about Judy's adventure plan. "You're going to try and have an adventure each month for 2004? What else are you planning?" They were live on the air.

"I'm going to Walt Disney World the first week in February...I'd like to take a train ride somewhere...maybe sky dive...whatever!" Judy was having fun thinking of the possibilities.

"Hey that's great...best of luck to you...we'll get that song out for you. And thanks for calling in." Jane hung up, but Judy heard her say on the air, "Wow, I want to meet this gal! I'd like to be her friend...maybe she would take me on her adventures, too!"

The song she requested played: *I Want to Do It All* and Judy joined in singing, scalpel in hand just doing her job. There was a sense of excitement inside her knowing she was starting her adventures that night.

"What does one wear to a Rodeo?" Judy wondered as she stood and pondered over the selection of outfits she had laid out on her bed. "I want to be comfortable...and it is very casual..." She decided on jeans, a white long sleeved T-shirt and a plaid shirt over it. "That'll work."

The indoor arena was already starting to fill as Judy scanned the selection of seats trying to determine where would be a good place to sit. Her insecurities started creeping up on her and suddenly she felt very alone.

"You can do this, Jude!" she thought to herself as she took a deep breath and walked up the row of bleachers to an empty area.

A family sat next to her with two small children. There were other couples seated around her. Judy sat there alone, but confident, feeling a little proud of herself for being there…alone. She watched the cowboys as they prepared for the performance. Each of them had their own style of attire and rituals for preparation.

The show was great and the rodeo clowns entertaining. She was glad she came. Jane and some others from KPGY were standing a few rows below her. They were getting ready to broadcast live from the arena. There was a break in the performance so Judy decided to go introduce herself and say hello.

"Hi…Jane? I'm Judy…the one who called in this morning planning a new adventure every month? I just wanted to say hi…"

"Hey! That is so cool! And this is your first adventure, huh? Well, I hope you have a good time tonight!" Jane shook Judy's hand but was busy trying to get equipment set up.

Judy smiled, "Thanks, I think I will." And she went back to her seat above them.

After the Rodeo the crowd moved across the gravel drive to another indoor auditorium where the dance was held. Judy's heart was pounding with anxiousness as she approached the building.

"I could just leave now…after all, I did do the Rodeo thing…" she thought to herself as she stared at the flood of people entering the building, "What am I doing here…"

"Judy? Judy, is that you?" A voice called out from crowd beside her. It was Amy and Andy from Shilo, friends of Jim along with another couple.

"We haven't seen you in so long…I almost didn't recognize you!" Amy said as she approached her. "You cut your hair…I like it."

Judy decided with her new life she needed a new look and cut of the long hair she used to have for a more sophisticated look and she was wearing her contacts instead of her glasses. "Oh, thanks…it was time for a change," Judy responded.

Amy looked around then asked, "Who are you here with?" They made their way to the door.

"Oh…I came alone," Judy answered as she presented her ticket to the guy at the door. He smiled and she smiled back politely.

"Really?" Amy sounded surprised. "Are you and Jim not seeing each other any more?"

"You know, Amy...we were just friends. I think he was planning to spend New Year's Eve with his guy buddies tonight...playing poker or whatever. We haven't been out in a while...he just wasn't right for me." Judy tried to present a confident front.

"I see," Amy said, "well, maybe you'll meet someone here tonight?"

"Maybe...who knows? I decided I won't meet people unless I get out so that is what I'm doing. You guys have fun tonight," Judy said as she walked away to another area of the room. She felt she wouldn't make herself mingle if she stayed in the safety of their company and tonight she was supposed to meet people.

Judy waved at the familiar face across the room. The poor guy waved back but looked puzzled, trying to place the face of the woman who just waved hello. As he approached her, Judy said, "Don't look so worried, Mark. You don't know me, but I feel like I know you. I listen to you everyday...all day...while I work." And she reached her hand out to shake his.

It was Mark Rivers, the station manager and owner of KPGY 94.5 radio in Northtown.

"I wondered..." he said as he shook her hand, "Good crowd tonight isn't it?" He glanced around the room proudly and then asked, "Have you been here before?"

Judy laughed, "No...this is my first time...my first adventure..." Mark looked surprised and then said, "Oh! You're the one who called in this morning...a new adventure every year! What a great idea! What is your name?" Mark was great a public relations. He was a young man that seemed older than his years. Judy felt she knew him well, having listened to him for so long. He had just recently married a month before.

"I'm Judy Braxtin...I recently moved to Northeast Nebraska...I live in Harvey. I listen to you guys all the time while I work."

"Where do you work?" Mark asked.

Judy laughed, "Well, I clone plants in the nursery in Clarmar. I work in a lab in isolation. You guys are my connection to the outside world!"

Mark looked surprised as most people are when Judy said she clones plants. She liked that about her job. It was different and interesting. "Are you here with someone?" Mark asked looking around them as if to see someone approaching.

"No...I came alone. I thought maybe I'd meet some people here. I'm not very good at the dating thing...and it's hard to meet people at my age unless you go to bars...which I don't. So I thought maybe this event would provide some interesting people to meet."

Mark was thinking, Judy could tell by the expression on his face and the look in his eyes. "We need to find you a date...come on lets dance and we can scope the area out." He took her hand and led her out on the dance floor.

As they danced he asked questions about her. She told him that she was divorced, was involved in a long term relationship that was somewhat dysfunctional and ended abruptly, and that she didn't like dating around. She shared her dream of finding someone to experience a great love with, like her parents shared, and how she wanted the whole package...love, romance, marriage and the happily ever after. Mark listened intently and with concern but always scanning the crowd. Occasionally he would pause and motion with his head in a direction saying, "What about that guy?" And Judy just laughed.

When they stopped dancing Mark said, "Listen, if you don't meet someone here call me at the station. Maybe we can do something to help you meet someone..."

Judy laughed, "Yeah, right...like you did for that one guy. You put him on a street corner and had women honk at him when they drove by...once if they were interested...twice if they weren't..."

Mark laughed, "Oh yeah...I forgot about that...but we wouldn't do that for you. A great looking gal like you shouldn't have any trouble finding a guy...but if nothing happens tonight call me!" And he went on his way, mingling with the crowd promoting his station.

Occasionally, she'd see him out of the corner of her eye pointing to some poor unsuspecting guy, as a candidate for Judy to approach...but she didn't. Mark then introduced Judy to a group of "singles" about her age who travel around to dances together. One woman in the group greeted her then proceeded to warn her to stay away from "her man". They were a peculiar group and Judy suspected they were into more "single" activity than she wanted and moved on.

"You want to dance?" The voice came from behind Judy as she stood watching the crowd. He was a tall, young cowboy.

Judy hesitated but then the thought reminded her, "You are here to meet people...take a chance...it's just a dance." And so she smiled and said, "Sure."

He was a student at a college in western Nebraska...in the sand hills. His father had a cattle ranch. He was young but said he didn't like women his age because they acted so immature. He was trying hard to convince Judy to let him take her home...it wasn't going to happen.

"No thanks...I appreciate the dance...but I'm really...I mean I just don't...well, you really need to go find a nice girl closer to your age!" And she smiled politely as she walked away.

The band announced the approach of mid-night and the New Year. The countdown began. Couples were cuddling, getting ready for that first kiss of the New Year. Suddenly, Judy felt very alone in the center of the crowd. She was tempted to call Jim...just to say "Happy New Year!" But she didn't. She felt sad...but she was glad she came. It was a start. She was learning a lot about herself.

No, she didn't meet Mr. Right that night, but she did step out of her comfort zone. She tried something new and she smiled as the crowd shouted, "Happy New Year!" While the band played *Auld Lang Syne*; and the crowd sang along, Judy thought to herself, "You did it, you made the first move. You'll be okay...it sucks to be alone, but you'll be okay."

The drive home from Melrose to Harvey was long that night. Although she felt good about her experience, she still felt empty inside. She longed for that one special guy...she just knew he was out there somewhere.

As Judy listened to KPGY she remembered her conversation and dance with Mark Rivers. "I just might take him up on his offer." She thought smiling. What do I have to lose? It was January 1, 2004.

* * *

"Mom, I want to contribute to your adventure planning. Let's take a trip to Colorado…just you and me. I have some time off from work. I'd like to see Grandpa and the family out there. What do you say?" Brad's voice sounded excited over the phone.

"How would Jen feel about you going?" Judy asked her son as she checked out the dates on her calendar for the possibility.

"She thinks it will be good. She is going to take the kids to go visit her dad next weekend. We could go then. It would just be a quick trip, but it would be fun. What do you think?" He sounded very convincing then added, "I'll pay the gas!"

"Hey, now that is an offer I can't refuse! It would be great to do something before I have to start classes again. I really want to see Grandpa and find out how things are going with him at Shirley and Terry's house. Sounds good! Let's go!"

As Judy planned for her quick adventure trip to Colorado, she decided to take Mark Rivers up on his offer and challenge KPGY to find her a date. She wrote him the following letter dated January 7, 2004:

Dear Mark,

I want to thank you for the dance at the Rodeo Ball on New Year's Eve. In case you don't remember me, I'm the one planning an adventure every month for 2004 and the one you were gracious enough to try and assist in my plight to meet some single people my age. Being new to the Northeast Nebraska area, it was my first time to Melrose and the Rodeo Ball and I had a lot of fun. Celebrating New Year's Eve alone was not   something I was looking forward to and meeting you, the other KPGY group and those you introduced me to helped.

On January 24 I will turn 49, thus explains my desire for a new adventure each month. I want to make this final year before I turn 50 a good one! Finding myself suddenly single at my age has been an adjustment. I have been out of the casual dating loop for a very long time and can't quite figure out how to do it. I lost my mom in September and after observing my father and her together in their last few moments before she died, I realize that I truly want that kind of love in my life someday.

Unfortunately, I haven't found it in my past relationships. I could really use (and would greatly appreciate) some good advice and direction.

I wondered if you at KPGY would like to join me in a new challenge and adventure to try and help me find the "perfect date" for my birthday. As a full time student at Northtown College, and also working full time, I don't have a great deal of free time to develop a social life. I could use all the help I can get and it might be kinda' fun! Surely, there are still some good single men out there who might like to "audition" for a nice date?

Having met me and talked with me I would hope that you found I am a very easy person to get along with. I've enclosed a couple of pictures of me to help trigger your memory and a few facts about me as well as some things I like in a guy. Let me know what you think of the new adventure and challenge and if KPGY would like to assist me in this.

Thanks again for the dance and KUDOS to KPGY! I listen to you every day while I work, at home and in my car. You guys are great! Keep up the good work!

Sincerely,

Judy Braxtin

Included in the letter was Judy's list of "Necessary" and "Preferred" characteristics as well as a summary about herself which gave a physical description and information on her likes; her dreams and goals. She mailed the letter the day she and Brad left for Colorado.

"Dad, you look so good. Shirley and Terry must be taking good care of you!" Judy said as she hugged her father. Shirley looked tired. Judy could tell caring for their father was taking a toll on her sister.

"How are you holding up, Shirley?" Judy hugged her sister who hugged her back strongly.

"I'm okay…I guess. How was your drive out?" And she hugged her nephew.

"Great! We stopped at every tourist trap along the way, just for the hell of it!" Brad grinned at his mother.

Bart shuffled his way to his easy chair and plopped down hard in it. Judy turned to her sister and spoke softly, "He's really failed since Momma died hasn't he?"

Shirley just nodded and added, "Yes, but he still makes the effort to get around. I don't let him drive anymore though. That was just too much of a worry."

Judy looked around the room and then asked, "Where's Sparky?"

Bart looked up sadly and said, "The poor little guy was getting so bad…we had to have him put down." And he pulled his handkerchief from his pocket to wipe his eyes and blow his nose.

Judy walked over to her dad and placed her hand on his shoulder, "I'm so sorry, Dad. He was a good little dog. Do you suppose he is running around playing fetch with Momma in heaven?" And they all laughed at the thought of that.

Brad and Judy enjoyed the visit with the family in Colorado. They made the usual stop to Casa Bonita in Denver, but it wasn't nearly as much fun with out the kids. They reminisced about the times they used to come there years ago when Lenny and Judy were still married and Brad, Alicia and Miranda were small. It was one of the good and happy things their family did do together.

As they watched the divers bravely dive from the cliffs to the pool below Brad said as he stared at the pool of water, "I need to visit Miranda before we go, Mom…okay?" Judy put her arm around her son and gave him a hug, "Sure, honey. We can do that before we leave in the morning if you like."

The climb to the top of the hill was a familiar one. "Wow, that tree has sure grown!" Brad said of the beautiful Ponderosa Pine which shaded the little grave.

Judy knelt and brushed the pine needles off the marker as her fingers traced the letters once again. She felt a peace this visit that she hadn't felt before.

Brad knelt beside her and said, "It never gets any easier, does it?"

Judy smiled at her son, responding, "Death isn't an easy thing, but it is a little less painful, now...I know Grandma is in heaven with her."

Brad placed the single pink rose on the stone at the feet of the little angel blowing a kiss. "I sure miss you Randi...he said as he placed his hand on his little sister's grave. I'll visit you again soon."

The little wind chime, encouraged to perform by the cold Colorado breeze, was playing softly and cheerfully in the branch above the small grave, as Brad and Judy walked slowly to the car: arm in arm and deep in thought.

Chapter 9
The Gathering

It was seven a.m. Monday, January 12, when the phone rang at Judy's house. "Who on earth is calling me this early?" Judy thought as she picked up the phone. "Hello?" She said softly, still trying to clear the sleepiness from her voice.

"Is this Judy...Judy Braxtin?" A somewhat familiar voice chirped from the other end of the line. Judy responded with a questionable "Yes..."

"Hey Judy! This is Mark Rivers calling from KPGY radio. How are you this morning?" Mark sounded excited, but then he usually did. He was one of the most enthused people Judy had ever heard on the air. He seemed to love his job.

"Oh, hi Mark..." she said suspecting the call was regarding the letter she wrote and suddenly wondering if she should have.

"I got your letter and I've got to tell you I was touched. You are a neat lady...we'd like to help you. What do you think about that?" Mark was seeking her permission to take the challenge she had presented in her letter. Was she ready for this?

"Okay...but what does that mean?" Judy asked cautiously, remembering the guy standing on the street corner.

"Well, I'd like to read the letter on the air to our listeners...not all of it just excerpts so they understand what the challenge is. How do you feel about that? I'd like to call you back…say about eight-fifteen, and we can talk live then. Would that be okay with you?" His voice was convincing.

"Sure, okay…I guess so…call my cell phone because I'll be at work then," Judy directed.

"Great!" Mark interrupted her, "Listen, I have to go for now, but I'll call you back at eight-fifteen. This will be fun…you'll see."

"Okay, I'll talk to you then…thanks Mark," Judy replied.

"Oh, no…thank you, Judy. Take care." And he hung up.

At eight-fifteen the cell phone rang as Judy waited at her desk in the lab. It was Mark and they were live on the air. "We're talking this morning with a listener who I had the privilege of meeting recently at the Rodeo Ball in Melrose. Good morning, Judy."

"Good morning, Mark," Judy responded as she listened to the conversation on the radio in the lab. "I sound weird," she thought.

"Judy you sent me a letter after our conversation that night and I'm going to share it now with our listeners so they understand the circumstances here…" And he proceeded to read parts of the letter to the listening audience.

"This letter really touched me and the staff here at KPGY and we want to help. It seems part of the problem with trying to meet other single people is there isn't a good place to do it. So we have decided to have a "Singles Gathering" this Wednesday evening at Barry's Bar-B-Q restaurant in Northtown. What do you think?"

"That might work. I love their food and the atmosphere is fun." Judy was nervous but tried to stay calm. All the while the little voice in her head was saying, "What are you doing?"

"So, Judy, who should we invite to this gathering? I see by the information you sent that you have specified an age group. You still want to put a limit on this?" Mark asked encouraging Judy to participate in the decision.

"You know, Mark…we should make this a gathering for anyone who is single and struggling to meet good people not just for me. Let's open it up to men and women age thirty and up…what do you think?" Judy was surprised at her confidence and decisiveness.

"Hey that sounds great, but we are going to post your picture on our web site so people can get an idea of who they are going to meet. And folks, I have to tell you, I have met Judy and she is a very attractive woman with a great personality. I hope you'll all come to Barry's Bar-B-Q this Wednesday night, say around seven o'clock p.m. to meet Judy. If anyone has any questions they can call us here at the station."

Mark was rapping up the conversation. "How's that sound to you Judy?"

"Sounds like a fun time, Mark. I hope to meet some good people…and I hope others do, too." Judy could feel the excitement inside her.

"Well, you never know, Judy. You may just meet Mr. Right at this gathering. Who knows?" Mark teased.

"You never know…" Judy repeated.

Then they were off the air and Mark said, "Thanks, Judy. Don't worry we won't give out any personal information to anyone or on the air or web site. I think this could be fun…what do you think?'

"I'm looking forward to it. Thanks so much Mark. I'm sure there are others who are feeling or have felt like I do about this whole meeting people/dating thing. I'll see you Wednesday."

There was a knock on the lab door and Susie peaked her head in," Was that you I just heard on the radio?" She laughed as Judy told her the story of how she and Mark danced at the Rodeo Ball.

"You are something else!" she said shaking her head, "I wouldn't have the guts! I hope it goes well for you."

The rest of the day KPGY announced the Singles Gathering often inviting singles from the Northeast Nebraska area to come and meet Judy at Barry's Bar-B-Q. The restaurant even offered a free drink to those who would come. The pictures that Judy enclosed in her letter were put on the KPGY web site and people were calling in commenting on Judy's letter and the great idea for a gathering.

"Mom, I can't believe you did this!" Alicia said as she poured a glass of tea for her mother, "A gathering for singles, huh? Gosh, maybe I should go," she laughed, checking out her mother's reaction.

"You're not old enough," Judy responded "It's for thirty and over…you're only twenty-nine…but it's probably close enough. You could come if you wanted to," Judy offered.

"No thanks, Mom. I think I'll pass…this is your party…I hope it goes well for you."

In Harmony, just off Highway 19, James MacDonnell was listening to KPGY on the radio in his shop. He heard the conversation between Judy and Mark and the plans they made for the gathering at Barry's Bar-B-Q.

James was a tall, quiet and handsome man. It wasn't that he was shy; he was just thoughtful and reserved. Seldom did he speak without thinking first. Something he had learned through experience. Life's hard lessons had molded his now admirable character. Working hard with his hands and with the heavy equipment he operated in his construction business is what he enjoyed. Several years back his marriage of many years ended when his wife left him for another man; a difficult thing to live with in this highly religious Catholic community. He got involved in a long term relationship after his marriage ended that was wrong from the beginning, but he felt obligated to continue. Encouraged by his children to end the affair and move the woman out…he did. It was the best thing he could have done as she was set to destroy him.

Loneliness was something he hadn't really thought about, although, he longed for that one special person to share his life with, but the memory of the painful past relationships helped to deter his thoughts. He just tried to work the feeling away, over scheduling his time and spending long hours doing his job. If he worked hard and was so tired when he got home he didn't have the energy or desire for loneliness any more.

"You should go…Dad, I'm serious…really…you should go. It would be good for you to meet some people," Margaret told her father as she finished trimming his hair. KPGY had been announcing the Singles Gathering nearly every hour for two days and the salon where James' daughter worked had it on.

The other stylists joined in the prompting saying, "Go…you're a good guy…she's looking for a good guy…you should go tonight!"

"I don't know…maybe I will," James said brushing the hairs from his sleeve and lap.

"What do you have to lose, Dad? If she's a dog, you can just leave and go home, or there might be other people you can meet…who knows? You need to get out. You need to do something besides working all the time." Margaret loved her father and she wanted him to be happy.

He was lonely…she could tell…and she knew he liked having someone special to share his life with. Caring for him and helping him redecorate the house when the "Evil One" (the name she gave to his live in girl friend) moved out was something she enjoyed. She did his grocery shopping and even cooked for him sometimes. She also helped with his laundry occasionally but didn't mind because she liked the fact that he seemed to depend on her. It made her feel important to him. Beyond that she loved him and could see he was lonely in a way she couldn't help with…except to encourage him at an opportune moment like this.

"What on earth am I doing here?" James asked himself as he looked around the room. There were several faces he recognized. Guys he knew from his old days of partying…desperate women who gazed upon him as if stalking their prey. He was uncomfortable.

"I should just leave while I can," he thought. The entry to the restaurant was packed with eligible men and women talking amongst themselves and looking and wondering.

Mark Rivers and Jane from KPGY were there broadcasting live and chatting with those around them. Each time the door would open all eyes would look toward it anticipating the entrance of the mysterious Judy who had instigated this whole experience. She hadn't arrived yet.

"Maybe she chickened out," James said to a man standing next to him.

"She probably can't find a place to park," he responded, "This place is packed!"

It was packed. No one was sitting down to eat until Judy got there and she was already ten minutes late due to an appointment in another town.

"I wonder what she is going to be like," James thought to himself. There certainly wasn't much of a selection of women at the gathering. They were either too young or way too old. Occasionally one would smile at James and he would politely smile back.

"I'm so sorry I'm late!" Judy said as Mark greeted her at the door, "I had an appointment I just couldn't get out of in Westbrook…oh my gosh!" She was overcome by the crowd as she walked into the room.

"Here she is everyone…"Mark said speaking live, on air, into the microphone, "Well, Judy what do you think?" And he put the microphone up to Judy's mouth.

"Wow! I'm amazed and my apologies everyone for being so late. Let's go sit and get something to eat and drink."

James stood back silently and observed Judy, his heart pounding. "She was worth the wait," he thought to himself, "I have to meet her." And he moved his way through the crowd, keeping himself close to her in order to be placed at the same table with her.

Judy was being escorted by Jane who introduced her to Paul, an older gentleman who was very short.

"You just stay with Paul and you'll be fine," she said as she directed them to a booth. Judy smiled down at him. Paul sat in the booth with Judy sitting next to him on the outside. James slid into the booth across from Paul and Chuck slid into place across from Judy and next to James.

It was awkward, but Judy tried to lessen the tension. She glanced around the men seated with her and smiled. Chuck was a little too straight forward. He stared continuously at Judy and it was really uncomfortable.

"I am newly divorced with two children. It's been really difficult. I need someone to help me through all this," he blurted out as he finished off his second bottle of beer.

"It would be good for you to work out those feelings," Judy said to him, trying to be courteous.

Then Paul spoke up, "I'm a widower. My wife died a little over a year ago. This is new to me."

"I'm so sorry for your loss," Judy said as she looked at the man sitting next to her. She determined he probably was a very sweet man, but he definitely wasn't over 5' 9" and she didn't think he met the age preference on her list either because he talked of being retired.

James just sat back and observed Judy as she attempted to be polite and interact with her suitors. When Judy directed her eyes to him he smiled and said, "Hi, I'm James. Are you doing okay?"

He had the most wonderful bluish-green eyes…"Like the color of the ocean…" she thought. They sparkled as he spoke to her. His handsome smile was framed with a closely trimmed Vandyke beard. And he wore his hair short and styled.

"Hey Judy, we need you to get up and mingle with the crowd. A lot of people have come here to meet you!" Jane's hand was on Judy's arm encouraging her to get up and move on.

Judy looked at James who smiled and shrugged. She hoped she would have time to get back to visit with him some more.

It was quite an adventure. There were some genuinely nice people but there were also some who were a little frightening, insisting that Judy give them her number so they could call her. She didn't though, politely responding "Why don't you give me your number and I can call you…" or "You can leave your name and number with the radio station if you'd like…" She was not prepared or interested in giving her personal information out to anyone in the masses as she wandered from table to table making small talk.

Occasionally she would glance back at the table where James was to make sure he was still there, hoping to get back there and visit some more. Then he was gone. She felt sad and frustrated, but out of the corner of her eye she saw him again. He stood back observing…waiting patiently…for just the right moment…observing her.

Gradually the crowd thinned out. Mark and Jane packed up and left. "I'll call you in the morning, Judy. I want to know how this goes for you," Mark said as he went out the door.

Judy looked at those left in the room. They seemed to have paired up and were enjoying their new acquaintances. Several couples left together. It was a good feeling knowing the gathering provided an opportunity for some to meet. James was still there, off to the side. The staff was cleaning up and getting ready to close the restaurant down. A few die-hard singles were discussing walking down the street to a small tavern close by to continue visiting.

Turning to Judy they said collectively, "You want to join us?" Uncertain what to say and wondering if she should, Judy looked over at James.

He stepped up to her and said, "I'll walk with you down there if you want to go."

Relieved, Judy smiled and said, "I'd like that." So they walked together along with the others to the tavern down the street.

It was a very cold evening…it reminded her of the evening just a year ago when her life had changed so dramatically. But there was no sadness in the thought…no longing or regret. She felt strong and fearless for having survived and redirected her life. The past was behind her now and she was moving forward toward a new beginning.

Once inside the tavern, Judy and James sat at a table with several other guys that James seemed to know well. They were much younger though and James teased them about even needing to go to a Single's Gathering at their age.

"Do you want something to drink?" James asked leaning toward Judy.

"A Diet Pepsi would be fine," Judy responded. She didn't drink much anymore since the West Nile and liked her life better with out it. James had a Diet Pepsi, too.

"You going to Sturgis again this year, James?" One of the guys asked.

James smiled and looked at Judy, those ocean eyes sparkling in the dim light. Then he said, "I don't suppose you like motorcycles?"

Judy's heart skipped a beat. She loved motorcycles, although she hadn't been on one in years. She remembered the thrill she had when the neighbor boy in Fairway had taken her for a ride once. It was so exciting. She replied, "I do…I mean, I think it would be fun to ride on one."

James winked at her and said, "Maybe Sturgis could be your August adventure."

"Maybe it could…" Judy said smiling back.

Their stare was interrupted by a card being tossed down on the table in front of them. Judy looked up at a guy from the gathering that put it there as he said, "Here…call me sometime." It was obvious that he thought he was God's gift to women.

Not wanting to be rude, Judy said, "Uh…thanks." As he walked away James smiled at her and shook his head. Judy just giggled.

James walked Judy back to the parking lot at Barry's Bar-B-Q. "I want to give you my number," she said to him as they stood shivering in the cold, "Do you have a business card that I could have?" She looked up into James' eyes. She liked the way she had to look up to him. He was so tall.

"Oh…yeah…but they're in my truck…" James said quickly.

"I'll walk with you to your truck so you can get it, okay?" Judy wanted to make sure she got that card. His business name and number was on the windows of the truck, "Mac Donnell & Son, Inc."

He reached into the cab and pulled out a card and handed it to her. She smiled, he smiled and neither of them knew what to do next.

Finally, Judy said, "I'd really like for you to call me."

James smiled and said, "Okay."

Then Judy turned and walked back to her car. As she drove out of the lot and pulled up to the light she looked at the card and smiled at the thought of James Mac Donnell. A horn honked from the vehicle to her left. It was James. He rubbed his hands together in a motion to signify how cold it was and smiled. She looked at him and a voice whispered in her head, "He's the one…he's the one." The sound of it took Judy by surprise because it was as if someone were speaking directly behind her into the base of her skull. It sent goose bumps down her arms and a shiver up her back. She determined it was her mother sending her approval.

As she turned to head toward Harvey the sky was clear and the stars were shining brightly. Then she saw it; a streak of bright light across the sky. "Oh, a falling star…" she thought to herself. "I should make a wish…" She thought of James smiling at her and his ocean eyes and she wished for him.

Chapter 10
Falling in Love...Again

"Hey, Judy! So how was it last night?" Susie asked as Judy walked past the green house outside of the lab. Ray was working over a table focused on dividing the roots of some plants that arrived in shipment. He glanced over at Judy and smiled.

Judy smiled back, "Good morning, Ray." There was a spring in her step and a new excitement in her heart.

"Must have been good," Ray teased as Judy walked by.

"I think it went well," Judy said trying to maintain her composure, "A lot of people were there and couples were leaving together..."

"What about you?" Susie gushed, "Did you leave with anyone?" She couldn't wait to hear.

"No, I didn't," Judy said blankly as she opened the door to the lab and stepped inside. Susie and Ray just looked at each other and shrugged their shoulders. Then Judy peaked out the door grinning from ear to ear, "But I might have met the man of my dreams!" And she went back inside and shut the door.

"That was quick!" Both Susie and Ray said together and then they laughed.

It was hard to concentrate. Judy kept looking at the card placed on the table beside the workstation. It was as if she couldn't keep her eyes off the name...James Mac Donnell...Mac Donnell & Son, Inc.

"He must have a son," she thought, "Or he works with his father…" She hoped she would have the opportunity to find out.

Right before she started her sterile procedures under the hood her cell phone rang. "Hi Judy, this is Mark at KPGY. So how did it go last night?" They were live on the air.

"Hi Mark. I think it went well. Could you believe the people there? It just goes to show how something like that is so needed in this area. I think some people connected. I saw a few of them leaving together," Judy was trying to sound professional.

"And what about you, Judy? Did you meet someone?" Mark was trying to get the scoop.

"I met a lot of people, Mark…" Judy laughed. She was stalling.

"But did you meet anyone special?" Mark rephrased his question.

"Well…there was this one guy…he's really sweet. He's the only guy I gave my number to and I hope he calls…I asked him to," Judy was hesitant to tell anymore. The rest was too special to blast to everyone on live radio.

"Really?" Mark sounded very interested, "You know you'll have to keep us posted if he calls so we know if we were successful or not at helping you out."

"Yes, I know…I will, Mark, thanks so much for last night. It was fun for a lot of people and several mentioned that they want to do another Singles Gathering again soon."

"Well, we just might have to do that. Have a good day and let us know!" As soon as Mark hung up Judy went to work under the hood; glancing often at the business card beside her.

"Hello?" Judy answered her phone on her way home from the night class in Westbrook.

"Hi, Judy…" The voice was all too familiar.

"Oh, hi Jim…how are you?" Judy tried not to sound like she was expecting someone else.

"I'm good. I know we haven't seen each other in a while, but I was wondering if you wanted to go out with an old friend for dinner on Saturday."

Judy hesitated.

"Judy?" Jim asked.

"I'm here, I'm sorry…okay, I guess it would be good to go out. We should probably talk anyway." Judy really didn't want to go, but she knew she needed to make some things clear to him and Saturday is as good a day as any.

"James probably isn't going to call me anyway," she thought to herself.

"Well, ok then, Judy I'll pick you up about five-thirty?"

"Okay, Jim…see you then." And Judy ended the call. Sadly she thought about the night before and those beautiful ocean eyes.

"Oh, James, I wish you'd call!" she said out loud.

The drive from her night class was long. Judy was tired. Even though she was feeling much better, she still noticed that she had a tendency to tire easily. When she got home there was a message on her house phone that showed a missed call.

"Oh my gosh!" she said, "That could have been him!"

She picked up the phone and called *69 to see what the last number coming in was. It was his cell phone! She was ecstatic but frustrated because she didn't know if she should call back or wait and see if he would call her again. She decided she would wait for him to call. She didn't want him to think she was chasing after him. She did that enough with Jim when they first went out.

"If he's interested he'll call you," she said to herself as she sat and stared at the phone.

"Hello?" Judy said trying not to sound too anxious.

There was a soft voice on the other end of the connection that said, "Hi, how are you? This is James…James Mac Donnell."

"Oh, hi James. I've been thinking about you, I'm glad you called," Judy hoped that wasn't to presumptuous to say.

"You have?" His voice was tantalizing and smooth, "What were you thinking?"

Judy was speechless.

"I'm in trouble now!" she thought.

"Ummmm…well…I was thinking that I hoped you didn't lose my number or something." Judy was nervous.

"I see…" James was calm and his words were soft. "How was your day?" he continued.

"Me…oh my day was…fine…busy…work and school." Judy wanted so much to sound sophisticated but ended up sounding like a college girl. Judy suspected that James could tell she was nervous.

"School? A college girl, huh?" he said teasingly.

"Yep" Judy responded. She was feeling more relaxed now. How she loved the sound of his voice in her ear. It was soft and soothing, but strong and masculine. "I heard you on the radio this morning."

Judy was surprised, "You did? I'm so sorry…I mean…I never know when they are going to put me on live or not. I hope I didn't embarrass you." Judy could feel herself blushing.

James was chuckling, "How could you…you didn't say my name. You just said you only gave your number to one guy. When I heard that I realized that I had your number and that the one guy you were hoping would call was me…but I was planning on calling you anyway."

"Really? You were? I am so glad you did!" Judy responded.

"So, you want to go out with me on Friday?" He asked softly.

"Friday, yes that would be great…oh…" Judy hesitated.

"What? Is there a problem? We could go out on Saturday instead…" he was being so sweet and considerate.

"No…Friday's good…it's just that…well…I have this *thing* I have to do at the College…" Judy was not sure how James would react to the rest of her explanation. And she made that "date" with Jim for Saturday, but she knew more than ever now she needed to keep that date.

"A thing?" James repeated.

"Well, yeah…you see…Friday is the Alumni Basketball Game…and…well…I'm the mascot for the team…" Judy cringed anticipating his reaction.

"You're what?" he said not sure if he heard her right.

"I'm the mascot. I have to dress up in the Eagle suite and hand out candy to the kids during half time…but it's only for a little while. We could still go out if you want." Judy hoped he had a sense of humor.

"You're the Eagle mascot for the college?" he repeated, as if to make sure he understood correctly.

"Yep...that would be me. You see they couldn't get anyone else to do it so I volunteered. I thought it would be fun and I just can't let the little kids down now." Judy explained.

James laughed, "Okay, it's a date, then. Hey, I never went out with a mascot before!"

"Thanks, James. You can come to the game and then I'll sit with you when I don't have to wear the outfit. No one knows it's me in there. I'm glad you're coming." Judy still wondered if he would change his mind later.

"Man this outfit is warm!" Judy thought as she walked around the gym during warm-ups. The alumni committee wanted the Eagle to greet the kids before the game and then hand out candy at half time. She kept looking toward the door, wondering if her date would show.

"I wouldn't blame him if he didn't," she thought as she hugged a little girl who cautiously approached her. She gave hi-fives to the older kids and clapped as the team warmed up and made baskets.

Being a mascot wasn't unfamiliar to Judy. She was her high school mascot for one year only that time she was a Wild Cat...and the costume was a little sexier featuring a short skirt, ears, tail, and boots. It was more fun back then as she remembers it.

"Oh my gosh! There he is..." Judy said to herself as her heart skipped a beat, "He is soooo good looking."

James looked over to her and smiled a huge smile and shook his head. He walked by and said, "Nice outfit!"

And Judy whispered, "I'll be done in a minute...thanks for coming!"

"James, what are you doing here?" It was the Mattsons from Harmony.

"I didn't know you were an alumnus?" Mr. Mattson stated.

"I'm not…" James answered, "I'm meeting my date here." he said smiling.

"Oh really? Who is it?" Mrs. Mattson asked curious to know who that good looking, eligible man was seeing.

James grinned, "She's over there…in the Eagle suit." And he pointed and waved. Judy waved back not knowing what she was the topic of conversation.

"Really…how nice," Mrs. Mattson mused and they walked away whispering to each other.

As Judy climbed out of the Eagle suite and into her regular clothes, she wondered if she looked as hot and frazzled as she felt. After a quick fix in the mirror she was ready to go sit with her date.

She was nearly out of breath when she sat down next to James on the wood riser in the gym. James looked at her and smiled. Then bent toward her and whispered, "I don't even like basketball!"

Judy smiled up at him, knowing he must have really wanted to see her after all. Then she said, "I bet you never had a first date with an Eagle before?" And they laughed.

They sat for the first half of the game and ate popcorn, not speaking much, although James did tell her about the Mattsons. They both laughed. Judy liked his quiet style.

"Well, it's time for me to hand out the candy!" She got up and smiled, "I'll be right back and then we can go. They want me in the hospitality room for pictures, but it shouldn't take long. I don't have to stay for the rest of the game."

James smiled and said, "I'll be here!" Judy was relieved to hear him say that.

They left the game and James took her hand as they walked down the sidewalk. His touch was tender, but firm and felt protective. Judy loved the way it felt.

It was cold again and they decided to leave her car at the College and go in James' truck. James opened the door and helped Judy step up into the cab. His truck was neat and clean inside and there was a Diet Pepsi in the holder. Judy started making mental notes about him. She wanted to learn everything she could about this man.

"Where would you like to go eat?" James asked as he turned up the heater, "You cold? It'll warm up in a minute...do you like Mexican food?"

"Sure. What ever you want is fine. I like Mexican food very much." He had no idea how often she had traveled to Mexico and enjoyed the cuisine there. She didn't care if he ever knew about that past life.

The restaurant had good Mexican food and James and Judy talked and talked and laughed together. Judy took constant mental notes of everything about him and wondered if he was doing the same.

After the meal James took Judy back to her car at the college, then he asked her, "You want to follow me to my house? It's kinda' on your way home." Judy could tell he didn't want the date to end any more than she did. "We can watch a movie."

Judy answered without hesitation, "Sure, I'd like that."

Then James teasingly said, "How do you know I' a good guy?"

Judy just looked into his eyes and said, "I think you are." And she smiled.

When they arrived at James' house, Judy followed him inside. It was a comfortable house and James removed his boots. Judy did the same.

"Now, let's see if there is anything on tonight," he said as he picked up the remote and sat on the couch. Judy sat down next to him her heart pounding with excitement.

James reached for her hand and held it as he moved closer to her on the couch. They started to cuddle and then James leaned toward her and kissed her. It was soft and sweet, as if he was afraid to be too passionate.

He looked at Judy and said teasingly, "My mom always said that kissing can lead to other things!" Judy just smiled.

They were so comfortable together and talked about some tough topics.

Judy decided to just put her cards on the table, "I need to let you know that I am serious about commitment in a relationship. I don't mean to frighten you, but I think it is important that we be as honest with each other as we can from the very beginning. I am not into mind games and jealousy and control issues. I want what my parents had. Does that scare you?"

James took her hand. "I have made mistakes in the past. I believe in marriage and love that lasts forever. I didn't have that, but I'm not afraid of that."

They talked about their past relationships, personal struggles and battles. There was total honesty established at the beginning. No games. They both knew what they wanted.

Judy learned a great deal about James that first date, but the most important thing she learned was that he was sincere and she trusted him. More than she ever trusted anyone else in her life. He was a gentleman, but not afraid to show his affection.

"You want to do something tomorrow night? Or do you have a date with your other boyfriend?" James asked her teasingly.

Judy smiled and said, "As a matter of fact I am meeting with Jim tomorrow, and it's important that I keep that date because I need to talk to him."

James was quiet but his affection never faltered. "What do you need to tell him?" he asked gently.

Judy looked into James' ocean eyes and said, "I need to tell him that I have met someone I am very interested in developing a relationship with and that I don't want to see him again."

James kissed her tenderly and whispered, "I'm glad...I feel that way, too."

Judy knew Jim would be coming soon. She needed to hear James' voice again. She needed the reassurance from him that what she felt regarding their relationship was also what he felt. That everything they discussed the night before was still true. So she called James. He was so sweet and calm. He gave her the assurance she needed and told her to call him later that night. Then the knock came on the door.

"Hi, Judy!" Jim said as he entered the house. Dottie greeted him and he patted her head. Then he looked up at Judy and said, "You look great." And he greeted her with a light kiss. "I thought we'd go to Westbrook to eat if that is okay with you."

Judy grabbed her coat and locked Dottie in the studio. "That's fine." She was anxious to tell him about James.

On the drive to Westbrook she told Jim about the Singles Gathering at Barry's Bar-B-Q with KPGY and how it all came to be. He said that it sounded like a good time.

When they got into the restaurant he asked, "So, did you meet any one there?"

Judy smiled and said, "As a matter of fact, yes. Yes, I did. That is why I wanted to talk to you tonight, Jim."

Jim looked sad but just kept smiling.

"His name is James Mac Donnell and I am very interested in getting to know him better and he feels the same way. We are going to date each other…exclusively. I won't be seeing you anymore."

Jim looked up from peeling the label off his beer bottle, leaned toward Judy, and said, "I am so-o-o happy for you, Judy. He sounds *perfect* for you!" Jim was such a nice guy…it drove Judy nuts!

"I'm glad you feel that way. I am very happy. He really is a great guy," Judy responded.

Then Jim took her hand and said, "He better be because I don't care how big he is…if he hurts you I'll kick his ass!"

That was a shocker…Judy had never seen that side of Jim, but there was no doubt he meant it. And then he cried. They both cried. They had made some history together, even though Judy had no idea what it meant.

They finished their dinner and Jim took Judy back to her house in Harvey. They held hands silently on the drive back. When Jim walked her to the door he looked into Judy's eyes and said, "I want you to be happy…you deserve all the happiness you can find. I really care about you, you know that…right?"

Judy smiled…poor Jim, was he trying to convince her or himself? "I know you care, Jim. You are a nice guy and I hope you will find your happiness someday, too." Then he kissed her goodbye. It was a long, soft, passionate kiss, but it was a kiss of goodbye and Judy felt a sense of relief and no regrets.

Although Judy was glad that the relationship with Jim was over, it was still a very emotional experience and she felt drained. She needed to talk to James, so she called him. "Can you come over, please?" she said. There was an urgency in the tone of her voice and James could sense it.

"I'll be there in twenty minutes," he said.

When James arrived he greeted Judy with a gentle kiss, put his arms around her and held her close. Judy buried her face in his chest breathing in the smell of him and absorbing the sensation of his arms around her. She was where she was meant to be.

"Let's go for a drive." James said as helped her with her coat and gently guided her out the door. They drove through every small town between Harvey and Harmony along Highway19.

James had lifted the arm rest and console between them so Judy could sit close to him. As they drove, he shared stories with Judy of his youth associated with each town. It was his way of introducing her to his past. Judy wondered what it must be like having always lived in the same area all your life. He had so much history and a large family in the area. He took her by homes in the small towns saying the names of those who live there and a home in the country he lived in as a boy, where his father still farmed.

"You didn't decide to farm?" Judy asked has she looked at the snow covered land where corn once stood. "Nah…I just wasn't the farming type. But my brothers farm with him so that is good. I always liked playing with my toy trucks and machinery in the dirt as a kid…now I still do; only they are a lot bigger," he said as he winked at Judy and smiled, his ocean eyes twinkling. He put his arm around her.

"So, Mac Donnell & Son…that would be you and your son?" Judy asked as she leaned into the comfort of his embrace.

"Yep…my son Marshall and I have the business together. He's a good kid…you'll meet him soon."

Judy felt a sense of joy when James talked of introducing her to his family. There was a tone of pride he expressed when he said it, which Judy had not experienced before with any other man. Dr.

Dickhead used to introduce her as his "office manager" or his "assistant" to people they met. Lenny just didn't bother to introduce her...his family hated her and they didn't have a lot of friends even for all the years they were married. And Jim...well...Jim didn't count. She never committed her life to him in any way. She didn't consider him as one of the three men in her life. He was a friend who helped her heal. Lenny was the first man she committed to, Dr. Dickhead was the second and James would be her third.

"Three's the charm..." Judy thought to herself as she smiled up at James sitting next to her. How she enjoyed sitting next to him in the passenger seat. Already, her feelings for him surpassed the feelings she had for the others.

They arrived at his house which sat just outside of Harmony on Highway19. Judy felt emotionally tired and her eyes were tender from crying earlier with Jim. They both removed their coats and shoes and James said, "We'll just relax for a while, okay? Maybe there will be a decent movie on..." and he sat down on the sofa and motioned Judy to sit beside him.

Judy cuddled up next to James, his arm around her shoulder. She was tired. They were both tired and the sofa was too narrow to lay on comfortably so James got up and said, "Here, get up a minute. We might as well be comfortable." And he pulled the cushions off and opened the sofa into a bed.

They laid on the bed with their arms around each other, watching some mindless movie and dozing off. "Let's get some sleep, dear," he said as he kissed Judy gently and he shut off the movie.

There was no sex, but there was an abundance of love between them, as he held Judy in his arms and she listened to the sound of his breathing until she was certain he was asleep. Then he rolled over to his stomach, reaching for her hand saying, "How's my honey?" The words melted Judy's heart. It felt so good lying there next to him...so right.

"He's the one..." she whispered to herself before drifting off to sleep.

"How's my honey this morning?" James said as Judy opened her eyes. Judy smiled she really liked the sound of that. "I'm good," she answered smiling.

James put his arms around her, "This feels so right, doesn't it?" And he gave her a kiss. "I suppose I should get you home or Dottie will wonder what happened to you."

Poor Dottie, she was left there all alone. Judy was feeling guilty for not being there for her more and was struggling with the thought of maybe finding her a better home with someone who would be there for her more or maybe someone with children. It would be a very difficult decision to make because Dottie had been a good companion for her when she was alone. But Dottie needed extra attention that Judy couldn't give her.

It was Sunday morning and very early when James took Judy home. Dottie greeted them happily as they entered the house. She had managed to get out of the studio room overnight and ransacked the rest of the house.

"Naughty Dottie!" Judy said scolding the little dachshund, but picking her up to hold her.

"I'll call you later. You should try and get some more sleep," James said as he kissed Judy gently.

"I probably will take a nap later. I want to go to church this morning, and I obviously need to clean up this mess!" Judy put the dog down and hugged James closely, "Thank you for last night…for being there."

James smiled and kissed her forehead. "Talk to you later." And he left out the door. When he got to his truck he looked back and Judy blew him a kiss. James smiled and waved.

He called later that evening, "Hi…how's my honey?" His gentle voice caressed her heart. "Did you get some rest today?"

"I'm good…yes, I took a nap," she said softly, "It was so good waking up with you this morning."

"Yes it was," James responded, "I want to take you out for your birthday on Saturday. Would that be okay?"

Judy was thrilled. "That would be wonderful! What are we going to do?" she asked.

"It's a surprise. I'll pick you up at six okay?" It had been so long since Judy had a *good* surprise from a man, the thought was exciting.

"What should I wear?" she asked, hoping he would give her a clue.

"Well, I'm wearing jeans…I usually do." James laughed.

"Okay, that helps! I'll see you on Saturday, then." She was so glad they had another date to look forward to.

"Oh, I'll call you before then!" James said confidently, "You have a good evening. I'll call again tomorrow."

It was Monday morning and Judy called Mark Rivers at the KPGY radio station as she had promised she would. First she spoke with Diane, the station office manager who then transferred the call back to Mark in the studio.

"Hi Mark." She said, knowing Diane had filled him in on their prior conversation.

"Hey, Judy! I hear you have some news for us!" And Judy realized they were talking live on the air again.

"I had a date, Friday, with someone I met at the Singles Gathering on Wednesday." She was trying to choose her words carefully.

"I understand that is name is James and he lives in Harmony?" Mark was having fun with this, but Judy wasn't sure how James would feel about having his name broadcasted live on the air.

"Yes, he is very special." Judy added.

"So how was the first date?" Mark asked. Judy paused before responding, but decided to have some fun with Mark and tell him about the date.

"Well, it was an interesting date. He asked me to go out with him on Friday, but I had an obligation to the college that I had to do…"

"Obligation? What kind of obligation?" Mark interrupted.

Judy had him curious now and was thinking ahead because James had asked her out for her birthday on Saturday and there was a basketball game that night which she planned on being the Eagle for again.

"Well...you see...he had to meet me at the college before we could go out on our date because...well...no one knows this...but I have been helping out as the Eagle mascot at the college sometimes for the basketball games."

Mark was laughing, "You're kidding! They know it now!" He said still laughing. "What did he think about dating an Eagle?" Mark was getting a huge kick out of the story.

"He was really great about it. We had a nice date afterward. And he wants to take me out for my birthday on Saturday."

"Hey, this sounds serious..." Mark was still chuckling.

"Well...I have a bit of dilemma. You see, I was going to do the Eagle thing again on Saturday, but I just don't think it would be fair to him to make him sit at the game while I am being the mascot again...so...I was wondering...if Buckwheat, your stunt guy, would be interested in filling in for me as the Eagle so I can go out with James for my birthday? We could make it another Singles Gathering."

Mark loved the idea and so did the college. It was great publicity for them both. Mark announced it as another Singles Gathering on the radio and the college would provide free passes for everyone who came to the game.

James called Judy every night that week. "Why don't you stop by the house on Thursday after class? Marshall will be there and Margaret is making chili. I'd like for them to meet you," he asked her one evening.

"Okay," Judy said nervously, "Should I bring anything?"

"Nope, just yourself. It will be fine, don't worry." James could sense the nervousness in her voice.

Judy entered the house knocking politely on the door. "Hello? Anyone home?" she said as she entered the kitchen.

Margaret and Marshall were seated around the kitchen table with their father and James rose to greet Judy, "Hey everyone, this is Judy...Judy Braxtin."

"So you're the one who keeps my partner out so late!" Marshall said teasingly and he reached to shake Judy's hand. He was tall, even taller than his father and thin. He had piercing dark eyes and a mouth that seemed to find it difficult to smile.

"Don't mind him…" Margaret said as she stirred the chili on the stove. "He's often rude to our guest!" she said, smiling then continued, "It's good to meet you. We've heard a lot about you, both from Dad and the radio station."

Margaret was a pretty girl, in her early twenties, and reminded Judy of what her Miranda may have been like if she had grown into a young woman. She had that sense of confidence and boldness that Miranda often presented. Judy suspected she could be somewhat stubborn, too and smiled at them both.

"The chili smells wonderful, Margaret. Can I help you with anything?" Judy asked.

Margaret quickly responded, "No…it's all under control. Just sit down over there and relax. I hear you just came from classes at the college…what are you studying?"

Judy took the chair beside James who took her hand and gave her a reassuring smile. "My major is business management, but I really love to write and paint." Judy was nervous.

"I draw some," Margaret said, "So, Dad says you have a birthday on Saturday. How old will you be…if you don't mind me asking?" Her dark brown eyes were focused on Judy's reaction.

Marshall put his head down shaking it back and forth in amazement at his sister's frankness.

Judy just laughed, "I don't mind…I mean KPGY already announced it over the air to everyone…I'll be forty-nine."

"She's an older woman!" James said with a gasp and they all laughed. James would soon turn 46. He gave Judy a hug.

"The chili is ready," Margaret said as she took some bowls from the cabinet, "Help yourselves. There's cheese to put on top if you like and crackers on the table."

As Judy ate the chili she wasn't sure what James' children thought of her. Marshall seemed receptive, but it was hard to tell with Margaret.

"I guess time will tell." She thought to herself, but it didn't matter. She and James had discussed this and decided that they are dating each other, not each other's kids. Their children were grown adults who had their own lives to live and James and Judy had theirs. They weren't seeking their children's approval nor did they need it.

"You seem to have a good relationship with your kids." Judy said as they sat in the living room watching another bad movie that just happened to be on T.V.

"You haven't even met my other daughter, Molly. She and Margaret are twins, but not identical. They really don't look anything alike at all," he said as he stepped over to the shelf picking up a picture of Molly and handing it to Judy.

There was a definite difference in the two daughter's appearance. Margaret was tall and thin with a long torso and short legs. She had short dark hair that was highlighted with blonde streaks. Although she appeared to be outgoing she seldom smiled and didn't seem to be very warm.

Molly was short and slightly overweight but had a beautiful warm smile. Her eyes were light like her father's and she and the man in the photo were cuddled together affectionately.

"She lives in Texas…her husband, Tim, is in the Navy."

Judy looked at the picture of Molly and Tim which was taken at their wedding and commented, "She is looks very happy. Is it hard having her live so far away?"

James looked at the picture fondly saying,"Not really, she calls often and comes home once in a while. I don't get down to see her that much though."

It was obvious he missed her. It was getting late and they both had to work in the morning. "Well, I suppose I should head for home." Judy wanted to thank Margaret for the chili, but she had already left. Marshall had gone outside to the shop to check on the equipment for tomorrow's jobs.

"Tell the kids bye from me and tell Margaret the chili was really good. I'm glad I got the chance to meet them. I'm anxious for you to meet my kids too…well, two of them anyway."

James walked Judy to her car. She put down her window as he bent down to give her a kiss. "See you Saturday," he said, "Thanks for coming!" She waved good bye as she turned out of the driveway onto Highway19 toward her home.

Chapter 11
The Birthday Gift

It was Saturday morning. Judy woke up early to clean her house and do laundry. Cheryl called from Washington and sang happy birthday to Judy over the phone. They talked for about an hour. Judy told her all about James and how they met. Cheryl was genuinely happy for Judy. Shirley called from Colorado with greetings for a happy birthday next also giving their dad the opportunity to say happy birthday to his baby girl.

"Happy Birthday, Judy" he sang to her cheerfully, "How are you doing, honey?"

Judy loved the sound of her father's voice. It took her back to that simpler time when she was little sitting with him on the cellar steps cracking open walnuts, or swimming at the Briarwood pool.

"I'm good, Daddy. How are you doing?"

She heard him sigh, "Oh…I'm fine. It's so different now. But I'm happy to be here with Shirley and Terry. Did you hear we had to put Sparky to sleep?" He had forgotten that he told her.

"Yes, Dad. I'm sure you miss him, but he was pretty sick, you know."

Bart sighed again, "Yes, I know."

Judy told her father all about the man in her life and what a great guy he was. She assured him he was a gentleman and told him about his the work.

"I am so happy that you have met someone. He sounds like he could be a good guy. I hope I get to meet him soon. Well, Shirley wants to talk now, so have a happy birthday…I love you…God bless you, honey." Judy could hear the receiver change hands in the background.

"Hi, Judy, it sounds like you have met someone new. What a story to have met through a radio station! You'll have quite a story to share someday with your grandkids!" Shirley said laughing, but then her tone changed, "Listen, Daddy is doing pretty good, but he is showing signs of getting more confused. I'm sure it's just the stress of losing Mom and he'll get better with some time, but I just wanted you to know. He talks about wanting to come back to Nebraska someday. That might be something we'll need to check into eventually." She was whispering, "He's okay for now and we're managing all right. I just wanted you to know…but don't worry about it! You have a great birthday today! It's your last one before you hit that half-century mark! Enjoy!"

Judy laughed with her sister and assured her she would, but before saying good bye she said, "Thanks, Shirley for taking such good care of Daddy. I wish I could be more help. When ever you think I should start looking into places for him here, you just let me know."

"Happy birthday, Grandma!" Maggie Lu was excited as she ran into the house with Dottie chasing after her.

Judy reached down and picked up her granddaughter, "Thank you sweetie!"

Maggie Lu presented her with a card. Alicia gave her mom a hug. "She has been so excited about bringing that card over to you."

"Where's Alex?" Judy asked as she opened the card.

"He's with his dad this weekend," Alicia replied.

Maggie Lu added, "I don't have a daddy to go to like Alex."

Judy glanced at Alicia who responded, "She's been doing that a lot lately. It's as if she just realized the fact that her father isn't in her life."

Alicia had Maggie Lu from a second marriage that was even shorter lived than her first. She seemed to have the same luck for choosing men as her mother did...until now.

"So tell me about this guy that you met?" Alicia said as she sat down at the kitchen table. "Is he a good guy?" she stated seriously.

"Alicia, he is such a good guy. I'm so anxious for you to meet him. I really think he is the one." The words flowed from Judy's lips effortlessly.

"What do you mean 'the one'...I mean...how can you possibly know that, Mom? I mean...really...you barely know each other!"

Judy was surprised at her daughter's reaction. "I just do...we both do...it's just the way it is..." Judy tried to explain.

"Mom! You can't be serious? How can you be sure...I mean...*really* sure. Aren't you afraid of getting hurt again?" And Judy realized that Alicia wasn't speaking out of fear for her mother, but fear for herself.

She sat down across from Alicia and took her hand, "I just know...I can't explain it...and you will know, too, someday..."

Alicia pulled her hand back, "I am not the least bit interested in finding a man!"

Judy sighed, "I realize that...and that is fine...but whether you accept it or not...I have...and he is wonderful. I'd like you to meet him." Judy could tell that Alicia was having difficulty accepting the idea that her mother might have really found someone special.

"I'm not sure I'm ready for that again, Mom. It was strange seeing you with Jim...you thought he was a nice guy, remember? Aren't you feeling the same thing about James?"

This was harder than Judy anticipated. "Listen, honey. I know this is hard, but I know what I am doing. I have never been so sure of something in all my life. There is just something about him. I know I can trust him. I'm not seeking your approval, but I hope you will understand when you do meet him someday...okay?"

Maggie Lu entered the kitchen carrying Dottie in her arms. "See my baby!" she said laying the dog on her momma's lap.

Alicia patted Dottie and saying, "You can stay here, girl…I'll protect you!" Dottie wagged her tail in appreciation.

Then Alicia smiled at Judy and said, "Mom, I'm happy for you. I can see you are happy…and that makes me happy. I'm sure James is a good guy, if you say he is. I'll try not to worry about it any more. Does Brad know?"

Judy realized she hadn't talked to her son since she met with him at that dental appointment in Westbrook the night of the Singles Gathering. That was the reason she was late. Brad had asked her to go with him to listen as the dentist explained the procedure he was going to do to correct the damage to Brad's teeth. He would need oral surgery.

"I haven't told him about James yet. I will though. I think he'll like him."

Alicia put Dottie on the floor and then took her mother's hand saying, "Just remember, Mom, after what happened on the lake he is a little protective of you." The scene of that night flashed in Judy's mind…the gun, the fighting, the fear and cold of it all.

"I know, I know…"she said as she thought, "…it will be okay, thanks." And she squeezed her daughter's hand.

When Alicia and Maggie Lu left, Judy treated herself to a warm bubble bath with candles and soft music. She put soothing cucumber pads on her eyes and a treatment mask on her face. She just wanted to relax and anticipate the evening that she and James were about to experience. He was coming to pick her up between five-thirty and six. She had no idea what they were going to do. It was a surprise and she hadn't had a surprise (a nice one) from a man in a long, long time.

"What do I wear for a surprise?" she said to herself as she searched her closet, "I want to look nice but everything feels tight!" She had gained back some of the weight she lost while sick with West Nile. "Hmmmm…I want to look sexy, but attractive. Think I'll wear my red sweater and black jeans with my black leather jacket. That should work. I can even wear my two inch heeled boots because James is so tall!"

Judy laid out the items on her bed. She noticed the message light flashing on her phone. "Someone must have called while I was in the tub." She thought as she played the message.

"Hi Judy. This is Jim. Realized it is your birthday and just wanted to say have a happy one." Judy erased it with no emotion. Nothing was going to distract her from this night. It was time to get ready for her birthday surprise.

James arrived looking incredibly handsome. They kissed and he walked her out to his pick up. Dottie watched from the window as they drove away. He had the console up so she could sit close to him.

"So do you feel any older?" he said with a smile.

"No...I feel great. Maybe I'll feel differently next year when I'm fifty," she said laughing.

"Have you ever eaten at The Brewery in Dover?" James asked as they headed south on Highway 18. James had lived in Dover briefly after his divorce from Peggy, the mother of his children. He met Marlene while he was living there. Marlene was the woman he had lived with for several years. Their relationship had ended a little over a year ago.

"No, I'm not familiar with anything in Dover since I spend most of my time in Northtown because of school. Is it a good place to eat?" Judy wondered if he had taken others there before her.

"I guess so...my kids took me there once for my birthday. It's kinda' neat inside. I think you'll like it."

As they approached the old remodeled building and parked, James put his arm around Judy and gave her a tender kiss. "Are you hungry?" His eyes were staring right into her soul.

"A little..." Judy said softly.

"Then let's go in!" James went out his door and opened passenger door for Judy and helped her step down from the truck. They walked hand in hand into the restaurant.

"Reservations for Mac Donnell," James addressed the host at the counter.

"Yes sir, right this way," he replied.

They were seated at a table and the server approached them and turning to James asked, "Are we celebrating anything special tonight?"

James winked at Judy across the table and replied, "Yes, yes we are. It is her birthday." And he smiled. Judy was impressed that he made it a point to acknowledge her special day.

Glancing at the menus Judy looked up at James, "Have you ever had frog legs?" She had eaten them several times in Mexico and liked them.

"No, can't say I have…would you like some? We can order them for an appetizer if you want." One of the things on Judy's lists was "not afraid to try something new" and he wasn't.

She smiled. "That would be great. I've had them before. They taste like chicken." And he laughed.

The food was wonderful! At the end of the meal the server brought over a selection of beautiful and rich deserts for Judy to select from for her birthday acknowledgement. She chose a rich chocolate cake, which James willingly helped her eat.

"Let's see what they have playing at the movie theater," James said as he helped Judy step up in the truck, "I'm not sure what time they start." Then he reached back to the seat behind them and handed Judy a big ivory envelope.

It took Judy's breath away as she opened it and removed the card from the envelope. It was so beautiful. The outside was ivory with a gold and silver heart framed in gold. The back ground had raised lettering with the word "Sweetheart". The hearts were a cut out window and the background peeking from inside the card was lavender. At the top of the card in gold lettering it read "Happy Birthday". Inside was the following inscription:

I've never been the same
Since the day I first met you.
Thank you for being here in my life.
Thank you for all the joy you bring to my world.

And then he signed it:

Happy birthday, Judy. Hope you have a great day.
Love, James

Judy held the card, her hands trembling and tears filled her eyes. She looked over at James who was smiling and he whispered, "Yes, I did read the card before I bought it." Assuring Judy that what was written was truly how he felt. This sweet man actually felt the same way about her as she did about him.

"It's beautiful" She said as she stroked the raised lettering that read "Sweetheart"...yes, she was his sweetheart and she liked the way it felt. "Thank you, God," she said silently to herself.

Reaching in the back again he handed her a pretty box with a satin ribbon tied in a bow. Inside was a scented candle with a glass globe. The candle scent was Sweet Pea.

"Margaret helped me pick it out. I hope you like it," James said observing her reaction.

Judy was so touched and amazed that he made the effort to get her something, but she truly loved the card. "Thank you. It's perfect," she said still caressing the card...and it was.

The movie wasn't starting for a while so they drove around Dover and James pointed out where his younger sister lived. He drove past the house where he used to live, after his divorce, which was located on a lake.

"How funny that we both used to live on a lake," Judy thought as they passed by. That life on the lake seemed so far away. She wondered if James also had some fun times on his lake partying, boating, and fishing as she did. "A previous life," Judy thought.

"Well, it's about time for the movie, you still want to go? Whatcha' thinking'?" James asked giving her hand a gentle squeeze.

"Yes, I'd like that...I'm thinking how lucky I am," Judy answered, smiling.

They saw *Cheaper by the Dozen* that night a comedy with Steve Martin about a couple with twelve children. It was hilarious and she and James laughed together a lot. Judy was so happy that he liked fun movies and liked to laugh. It felt good to laugh again. She hadn't done much of that over the last few years.

"What do you want to do now?" James asked as he leaned toward Judy and kissed her passionately. They were parked on the street out side of her house.

"I know what I want to do, but I'm not sure if we should," she said softly between kisses. Then she looked him in the eye and said, "Can I trust you with my heart?"

And he looked her in the eye and replied, "Yes, can I trust you with mine?"

The decision was made and they went into Judy's house on the corner of Third and Grace Streets. Behind closed doors with Dottie lying quietly in the other room, James kissed Judy tenderly as he whispered, "We don't have to go any farther...its okay."

But they both knew what they wanted. Judy looked at him with tears in her eyes and said, "This is crazy...it's so soon, but...I love you, James. I really do."

James smiled, "I know, I love you, too." They were like two young lovers discovering the joy and pleasure of the first time.

"Will you still respect me tomorrow?" Judy asked as they kissed.

James responded, "Yes, will you still respect me?"

That is when she realized they both shared the same fear. That cold January night they chose to have faith in their new love and hope for their future together as they gave each other the best gift of all...love.

Chapter 12
When You Wish Upon a Star…

"Hi Judy…this is Ted." Judy was surprised that Jessica's husband would be calling her.

"Hello, Ted. What's up?" Judy was hurrying to get ready for work.

"I just wanted to invite you to a party this weekend for Jessica."

Then Judy remembered. "That's right! This is the big one isn't it?" Jessica was a year older than Judy.

Ted laughed, "Yeah, she's turning the big 5-0! I'm trying to have a surprise party for her, but you know Jess…she investigates everything. I think she might suspect what is going on."

Judy laughed. Jessica was one of the most curious people she knew. She was also very organized and structured. The garage sales they used to have we're planned for weeks. "Well, she hasn't called me yet to try and find out if anything is happening. And I won't tell her if she does," Judy said trying to assure Ted.

"Good, thanks…I hope you and your new guy will come…its Friday night at seven…the same place you and Jess went for Jim…well, the last birthday party you went to." Ted hesitated to bring up past feelings.

"Its okay, Ted. Jim was a good friend. I don't have a problem with it."

Ted gave a sigh of relief, "That's good because, you know, he will probably be there, too." Judy hadn't thought of that, but of course he would be there. He was Jessica's special "guy-friend" and she would want him there.

"It's no problem, Ted. I'd like for him to meet James anyway so he can see for himself what a great guy he is. I'm anxious for you all to meet him." Judy meant that with all sincerity.

"You sound really happy, Judy. I'm so glad…you deserve it. We'll see you on Saturday."

While at work Judy called Mark at KPGY to see how Buckwheat did filling in as the Eagle mascot for her and if there was a good turn out for the Singles Gathering. "It was good, Mark said. The crowd loved it and, yeah there was a large group there. How about you…how was your birthday date?"

"It was wonderful! He is a very special guy…"

Then Mark interrupted, "Who is this guy anyway?" He suddenly sounded somewhat like a protective brother. So Judy went on to tell him some basic information about James.

"Sounds like you two have really hit it off. Just remember, Judy…if you two should get married you'll have to invite the KPGY and staff to the wedding!" And they both laughed, but deep inside, Judy was looking forward to that day and, somehow, she knew it would come.

"Let's go to town and get a burger," James said as he rose from the couch, "The Deep Woods Bar has really good food…I'm hungry aren't you?"

Judy hadn't thought about eating. It had been a long day with work and school and she was glad to just be there with James relaxing. "I guess it is that time, isn't it? Ok, I could eat a good burger." So they drove into Harmony and parked at the Deep Woods bar.

"You realize you are the *mystery woman* here." He told her as they walked through the doors. Several of the patrons greeted James and smiled. Judy felt awkward and slightly uncomfortable with their stares. James introduced Judy to the owner and they ordered the burger special.

"I like your town," Judy said. It was obvious he was very proud of it and content to live there.

"It's a good town," he said as he sipped his Diet Pepsi.

They spent as much time together as they could during the week. James would call Judy every day. When it was icy and she had to drive to Northtown he would call to make sure she got there safely. It felt as if they had known each other for years. He agreed to go with Judy to Jessica's fiftieth birthday party.

"Hey, girl!" Jessica's voice called out across the room. "This must be Mr. Wonderful...hi, I'm Jessica, Judy's twin sister...don't we look alike?" Jessica said as she pulled Judy face close to hers.

James just smiled politely and turned to Judy saying, "You never told me you have a twin?" Then he winked and smiled. Jessica was having a good time opening up the ridiculous "over the hill" gag gifts and greeting her friends

"There's someone I want you to meet," Judy said as she took James hand and they walked toward the bar.

"Jim?"

Jim turned saying, "Judy! How are you?" He hugged her, and she turned toward James saying, "Jim this is James...James Mac Donnell. James this is Jim...Jim Sorensen." The two men shook hands politely and made some brief small talk. It felt good to introduce them. She wanted Jim to see how very happy she was with James and see what a great guy he really was. Although James didn't really know anyone there he never had any problem mingling in the crowd. They stayed until they noticed that the weather outside had turned bad. It was a typical Nebraska snow storm.

"We'd better get going," James said to Judy as she hugged Jessica.

"It's a long drive back to Harmony and we are supposed to go to James' parents tomorrow," Judy said to her friend.

"I'm so glad you came, Judy, and it was nice to meet you, too, James. I hope we'll see more of each other. Gimme' a hug!" Jessica was feeling the effects of her party drinks.

James smiled and hugged her. "I'm sure you will," he said as he helped Judy with her coat.

"Thanks for coming, guys." Ted said as he walked with them to the door, "Man, it is bad! You guys drive carefully!" James and Judy waved as they drove into the storm, back to Harmony and back to his house for the evening.

"So this is the woman who has stolen my son's heart?" James' father greeted Judy as she entered the house, "Hi! I'm Marshall, but everyone calls me Mac...you can, too. It's just too confusing now that there is a young Marshall around." He took Judy's hand and shook it briskly. It was easy to tell where James got his good looks. Mac was tall and had pale blue eyes that twinkled when he smiled.

"Mac, take easy on the girl! You don't have to shake her arm off!" James' mother scolded her husband, "It is so nice to meet you. My name is Laura. It seems you have made quite an impression on our son. Please come in, dear and have a seat. Would you like some tea?" Mrs. Mac Donnell was an attractive woman with green eyes, silver hair and a gracious smile. She was short in stature and reminded Judy of her own mother.

"I'd love some tea...thank you," Judy responded as James took her hand and they sat together on the flowered sofa across from his father.

"So, son...how is business?" Mac turned his attention to James.

"It's going well, Dad. We're a little slow right now because of the time of year, but we have some good things happening once the weather warms up," James replied confidently.

"Well, if it doesn't pan out you know you can always help us out on the farm..." Mac grinned and winked at Judy.

"Dad, I think you have plenty of help with the other boys in the family...you don't need me," James responded gently squeezing Judy's hand.

It was a good visit. Judy was thrilled to meet James' parents. "I'm so anxious for you to meet my dad and family someday."

"Oh, I will. Maybe we'll ride the bike to Colorado when the weather gets nice and I can meet your family out there. Would you like that?" James gave Judy a quick kiss before she climbed into his truck.

"I'd like that. Of course you'll probably meet them all when they come back for Mom's memorial service in the spring," she said as she scooted next to him and they headed toward Harmony.

"I will miss you." Judy said as James held her in his arms; his fingers gently caressing her shoulder. It was time for her February adventure.

"Nah, you won't," James teased, "You'll have so much fun down there... why would you miss me?" And he kissed her on the nose and grinned.

"It *will* be fun," Judy said as she snuggled closer. "The kids are so excited to see Walt Disney World...I can't wait to go to Epcot. I haven't been there for years..." Judy had traveled there once with Dr. Dickhead for a convention. She was looking forward to seeing more of it than the bars of various countries. Back then she got yelled at for wandering off to purchase a souvenir magnet because some woman took over her spot at the British Pub where Roger was waiting. He also got mad at her when she wanted to sample the various foods telling her she'd get fat eating so much.

"Whatcha' thinkin'?" James voice was soft. He could tell Judy had drifted off into her thoughts.

Judy just looked at him and smiled, "I was thinking that visiting Walt Disney World with Alicia and the kids will be a whole lot more fun than it was when I went before."

James smiled back. He didn't ask a lot of questions about Judy's past life. It didn't matter to him. What mattered was the here and now and their future together.

"Grandma, LOOK!" Maggie Lu repeated this over and over as their days in Walt Disney World went on. They would go all day until the kids were so exhausted and started getting cranky.

"Grandma, will you go on the Buzz Lightyear ride with me again?" Alex asked for the tenth time.

"Sure, why not?" And Judy raced him to the waiting line.

Judy spent her days with Alicia and the kids and in the evening she would walk the beautiful grounds of the hotel and find a quiet place to call James to see how his day went. They would have long talks and she would tell him about the incredible sights and rides.

As she returned to the hotel room Alicia was getting the kids settled in, "Where were you?" She asked. She sounded aggravated.

"I was talking to James on the phone…why?" Alicia still wasn't accepting the fact very well that her mother was in love.

"Oh…I just wondered…the kids were wondering…I guess," Alicia responded without looking up from the magazine she was glancing through.

Judy hugged her daughter. "This has been a wonderful trip and what an incredible experience for the kids. I'm so glad you invited me to go with you. This is the perfect adventure for February!"

She could tell Alicia needed some assurance and appreciation. Raising two kids alone is a difficult and demanding job. Sometimes things just get to you. "Thanks, Mom," she said as she hugged her back.

The climax of the trip to Walt Disney World was the fireworks at Epcot. Judy remembered it was a fantastic exhibit when she had been there previously but not like that night when they were there. It was truly a wonderful experience and memory. The song, *When You Wish Upon a Star,* echoed across the park.

"I hope James can see this someday," Judy thought to herself. "He would be amazed!"

The year 2004 was off to an incredible start. Judy's adventures had just begun. In March she went to a spiritual retreat associated with James' church. It was a couples program. James had gone with the men in February.

"Would you be interested in going with the women in March? The other wives of the men in my group are all going in March. Once we do this then we can go to the meetings together with other couples. I think you would really enjoy it." James was so sincere and Judy had noticed a change in him since he attended his weekend. He seemed more focused and content.

She had gone on retreats before and always enjoyed the speakers and time to relax and regain a spiritual focus. She liked the way he included her as one of the "other wives". She was glad his focus was in that direction. They had discussed marriage on several occasions, but felt they needed to give their relationship some time. It wasn't so much for them as for their families. Although their families seemed to accept them as a couple, James and Judy felt they would want them to have a little more time in the relationship before they got married. It was still so new.

Judy looked at James and said, "Sure, Sweetheart, I'll go. It will be good for me to learn more about your church and meet some people." And so she went. It was one of the most incredible experiences she ever had. The speakers were wonderful and the prayer time was great. Judy formed friendships that she knew would stay with her for life.

After their weekend experiences, James and Judy became more conscious of where their relationship was headed and the importance of living it right. Judy had moved in with James because they wanted to be together always and in all things. They enjoyed sharing their lives. They wanted to marry, but James' faith prohibited it without annulments from their previous marriages. It was frustrating.

"Why don't we just run off and get married...just the two of us!" Judy told James one day thinking it was a great idea.

"I...I just can't do that," he said solemnly,. "I want my family there when we marry. I want it in the church. It's important to me."

Judy had no idea how important it was until he said it that day and she saw the look in his eyes. He was in a difficult situation; having been raised in a faith and church that he loves dearly, but unable to participate in it fully with the woman he loves, because of divorce. There was no easy solution.

"We'll figure something out," Judy said as she touched his hand, "There has to be a way somehow." But she wasn't sure how. Judy's faith was strong and she knew she could worship anywhere, but James truly loved his church in Harmony where so many of his family had attended and wanted to remain in it.

Judy didn't blame him. It was a beautiful church. The first time she went there with him it took her breath away. It was as beautiful as the Basilicas she had visited in Italy with its fresco paintings and statuary. The people were warm and caring there. Even though the services were more ritualistic than Judy was used to she understood the reason and discipline behind it all. She was comfortable worshipping there with James.

Their first year together was full of many family events that more than completed Judy's adventures every month. There were weddings and funerals for family and friends, including the memorial service for Judy's mother, Bonnie, in June. Judy took the train to Washington to visit her sister, wore her mother's clown outfit in a Fourth of July parade, went to a Mac Donnell family reunion, and rode on the back of James' motorcycle to all the way to Sturgis where they camped in a tent there. They visited James' daughter, Molly in Texas twice, and moved Judy's father, Bart, back to Nebraska to a care center close to Harmony so Judy could visit him often.

The best event took place in December. James decided to go to Omaha to the shopping center. As they passed the jewelry store Judy slowed down and holding James hand they walked together toward it. His hand was sweaty and he was nervous.

"Let's just go in and look," she said smiling up at James, "It won't hurt to look." James hesitated, but seeing the excitement in Judy's eyes surrendered to her leading.

"Is there something I can help you with?" The sales person behind the counter asked.

"No…no…we're just looking," Judy said, wishfully gazing at the sparkling rings in the glass cases around her.

"What do you like?" James asked her and Judy smiled knowing he was interested too.

"Something simple…two toned…and it would have to fit with my mother's gold band." Judy had requested her mother's wedding ring from her father because it was what she wanted when she and James would marry. Her father and siblings were happy to oblige. They liked James very much. Then they spotted it. It was just as Judy imagined. There was a single round diamond with four small round diamonds on each side, set in a two toned mounting.

"We'll look at that one," James told the sales person, taking charge of the situation.

Judy slipped the ring in her finger. It was so beautiful! "Oh, look...the four diamonds on each side can represent you and your three kids and me and my three kids and we're joined in the center by the single diamond...our marriage. It's perfect...I love it!" Judy was so excited.

"Are you sure? It isn't very big...I was going to get you one like that..." And James pointed to a huge diamond similar to the one his son had given to his bride.

"That's what I was afraid of, and that is why it is good we did this together. I am not the big diamond type. I like things simple. This will look really nice with Momma's plain gold band." She held it up for James to see.

The sales lady offered to let them look at the diamond under the scope to check its quality. James wanted to do that. Then she turned to James and said, "What about your ring, sir? What do you want?"

Judy and James had agreed to get a titanium band for him since he said he will always want to wear it, even while working, and titanium is virtually indestructible.

So it was done. They were engaged, although they agreed not to tell anyone until Judy's ring came in. It had to be special ordered since her fingers were so small.

Judy held James hand tight as they exited the mall. It was starting to snow...the first snow of the year. "Thank you!" she said, "I love you so very much!"

James smiled but looked concerned. "It's just so scary...I mean...what if I disappoint you..."

Judy hugged his arm close as they walked. "It is scary...but I love you...you could never disappoint me...it will be wonderful...you'll see."

James opened the door for her and kissed her saying, "I love you,"
As they drove back to Harmony, James held tight to Judy's hand.
"Are you happy?" he said as he squeezed her hand gently.

"Very!" she said smiling up at him, "Are you?"

James smiled and his eyes twinkled, "I really wanted to get you that $4,000.00 one!" And they laughed.

"Hopefully our annulments will go through easily and we can get married in the church. That could take some time you know." And he squeezed her hand again.

"I know…or we could get married in the church I was raised in and then when the annulments come through have our marriage blessed in your church?" Judy said, smiling, then adding, "Either way, we are getting married, but I want to enjoy being engaged for a while. I've never been officially engaged before."

She really hadn't. She and Lenny got married because she was pregnant. And Dr. Dickhead just led her on telling her he would marry her but never doing anything about it. Judy looked at James who was smiling.

"Whatcha' thinkin'?" she asked him imitating the way he asked her so often.

James smiled, "I was thinking how lucky I am to have you…and hoping you feel the same way."

"I do," Judy said and smiled at the nice sound of those two little words.

Chapter 13
Bless the Broken Road

"I got it! I got it!" The shrieks came from all directions behind Judy as she stood with her back to the group of single, eligible women anticipating the toss of the bridal bouquet. Judy closed her eyes; reflecting on the preparation and celebration of this event and who the lucky recipient of the bouquet would be.

It was exactly two years to the date that she and James met at the Singles Gathering at Barry's Bar-B-Q. There had been many changes in their lives. Judy had graduated from college and started writing and illustrating children's books. She enjoyed being able to work from their home and helping James with his bookkeeping whenever she could. In her spare time she made efforts to enjoy her engagement and wedding planning; attending bridal fairs with her daughter and purchasing bride magazines, but wanted to keep it simple. The ceremony needed to be unique to their circumstances and style. She wasn't into a lot of formality and wedding hype.

They would marry in the Episcopal Church in Northtown, as she was raised Episcopalian. She liked the little church, which was over 100 years old. It would be a simple, private ceremony with family members and a few friends. A catered dinner from Barry's Bar-B-Q would follow at the Harmony Auditorium and then an open reception. She would use silk flowers to make all the bouquets and corsages adding that personal touch to everything.

"What do you think of pink?" Judy asked James as she skimmed through another bride magazine.

"Pink? Really?" James wasn't sure if she was kidding or serious, but as he looked up from the paper he could tell she was serious. "As long as I don't have to wear it, I guess it is fine." Then he winked and smiled.

"Maggie Lu wants a pink flower girl dress...I don't know. Are you sure you don't want to just take off somewhere and get married instead of going through all this?" Judy was getting frustrated.

"Honey, you can do what ever you want for the colors, flowers and decorations...but I really do want a ceremony in a church with our families present," James stated and Judy knew he was certain about that. It was just one more thing she loved about him.

"Oh, I know, Sweetheart. I just have to ask once in while to make sure you're still in this all the way." She glanced up at him and grinned.

James sprung out of his chair and playfully tackled his bride-to-be on the sofa, tossing the bride magazine on the floor.

"You're stuck with me now!" He said as he pulled her close and kissed her.

Judy looked into his eyes and stroked the hair on the top of his head, "That would be a good thing!"

Their relationship was like that...easy. No hassles. Both of them had been through such difficult situations before so they knew the difference between what was worth getting angry over and what wasn't. Because of that, they never fought, never lost their temper with each other, and never intentionally hurt each other's feelings. It was natural for them to just talk about issues, to respect each other's feelings and handle things calmly, reserving their energy for loving each other tenderly and passionately.

It wasn't that their lives were free of turmoil. There were many situations that occurred, which would have stressed any developing relationship; conflict with their grown children (as often happens when families are blended), difficult decisions, business and work stress, and illness, but they worked through them together. It wasn't always easy to keep their focus on separating outside conflict from their personal life, but it worked for them. They listened to each other before taking the advice of others and they set boundaries of love to protect their relationship from outside influences. Although their families were important, taking care of each other was the priority. There were four factors that seemed to make the difference in their relationship:

Faith - knowing where to turn when they needed strength
Hope - believing that what is yet to come will be good
Trust - total and complete confidence in each other
Respect - genuine concern for each other's feelings

These four principles kept their relationship loving, strong and growing and helped to make preparing for the wedding less of a challenge for Judy. It was a second marriage for them both so she wanted it to be special but didn't want it to be too big. That was hard to control, since with James' family, everything was done in a big way.

"Have you picked out a gown yet?" James' mother asked Judy as they sipped their tea.

"I just don't know...I'm just not the wedding gown type. At my first wedding I wore muslin and carried straw flowers. Everything I look at has sequins and pearls and too much fluff! I have a picture in my head of what I want, but I haven't found it..." It was a source of aggravation for Judy. "I would be happy to wear jeans or maybe a nice suite of some sort."

"Oh, my! You wouldn't wear jeans...really?" Mother Mac Donnell couldn't hold back her shock at the thought of it.

"No, no...I wouldn't...although that is more my style. I'll find something that is simple, beautiful and comfortable. It's out there somewhere." Judy smiled at her soon to be mother-in-law who smiled affectionately back at her over her cup of tea.

Judy did find her dress. It was perfect. She and James had gone to visit his daughter, Molly in Texas and while they were shopping at a mall they walked by a dress shop. Judy noticed the beautiful formals in the display window and paused.

"Let's go in for a minute...I just want to look." she told James as she walked toward the store. Holding James' hand they walked in together.

There it was...hanging right there on the rack in front of them. It was ivory satin with an appliqué of light pink flowers and embroidered pale green leaves. There were a few delicate sequins tastefully scattered on the flower petals. The style was simple, but eloquent. Judy didn't want James to know she saw it.

"You know I'm not supposed to see your dress before the wedding so I shouldn't be here looking with you" James commented, as if he knew she found the dress, "I have some tools I want to check out in Sears...you want to meet me over there in...say...fifteen minutes?"

"Well, okay if you don't mind. I'd like to just look around here for a minute and maybe try some things on." As soon as James was out of sight she took the dress to the fitting room.

As she turned and looked in the mirror she knew it was just what she imagined in her mind. It was beautiful and it was on sale!

"Would you like me to put this in on a hanger and in a dress bag?" The young sales clerk asked as she carefully rang up the gown.

"No...No...just roll it up and put it in a bag...that will be fine," Judy said to the surprised clerk. She didn't want James to know she found her dress and she knew she could steam it out later.

When she approached James he looked at the bag asking, "What did you buy?"

"Oh...just something on sale. Did you find any tools you want?" Judy replied quickly.

"There are always tools I want...but do I need them...that's the question." He hugged his fiancé and took her hand. They left the mall with Judy carrying the secret in the bag.

* * *

"You look so beautiful, Mom!" Alicia said as Judy stepped out of the dressing room for the pre-wedding pictures, "The dress is perfect and I love the wreath of flowers in your hair. James is a lucky man!"

"Thanks, honey. You look beautiful, too. I'm so glad you are standing up with me. It's important for me to have you there to share my joy." Judy kissed her daughter on the cheek, knowing it wasn't an easy thing for her to do. There is just something strange about your parents getting married. Judy empathized with their adult children

"What about me? Am I beautiful, too?" Maggie Lu said as she twirled her long pink dress laughing. Little Faith was giggling and clapping her hands next to her, also dressed in pink.

"Yes, Lu Lu...you look beautiful, too. And look at you Faith! What a pretty dress? Are you going to help Maggie Lu today?" She decided to have a flower girl and an assistant flower girl. She wanted little Faith Hope to have a part in the ceremony.

Judy took her granddaughters' hands, "We better find your Grandpa James so we can get these pictures taken."

"He's in the church, Mom, with Marshall and the ring bearer...what's his name again?" Alicia said as they walked down the narrow hall way to the sanctuary.

"That's James nephew, Tyler. What do you think of him, Maggie Lu?" Judy asked her granddaughter.

"Uh...he's okay, I guess...for a boy!" And Maggie Lu wrinkled up her nose.

Judy walked into the church and James' face lit up when he saw her. He looked so handsome in his tuxedo. They met each other at the altar and he kissed her on the cheek.

"I'll wait to kiss you more completely once you are Mrs. James Mac Donnell," he whispered as he held her close.

Judy's mother had given her a pair of pearl earrings years ago. Bonnie had told her that Bart had given them to her when they were dating. Judy wore them that day. Alicia gave her mother a new gold locket as a wedding gift. Judy placed pictures of her sweet mother,

Bonnie, and deceased daughter, Miranda inside and it hung gracefully around her neck; close to her heart.

Judy was reciting the poem in her head, "Something old, something new, something borrowed…" Then she realized, "I don't have something borrowed!" she said as she waited in the foyer before the ceremony; her father and son standing ready at her side.

"Here, honey. You can borrow my handkerchief." Bart said as he handed his daughter the freshly folded hankie from his Tuxedo jacket. "I have a spare in my pants pocket!"

"Thanks Daddy!" She kissed his cheek and held tightly to his arm. His legs were getting weak, but he was determined to walk his daughter down the isle. Brad would walk with them assisting his grandfather into his place in the pew once they reached the altar, surrendering their daughter and mother over to James.

"Two of my favorite men beside me!" Judy said as she squeezed their arms glancing down the isle at James waiting for her at the altar…"Three's the charm!" She whispered softly.

The blue wedding garter tucked under her gown, around her right thigh, and given to her by her friend Jessica, completed the tradition of something old, something new, something borrowed, something blue.

The ceremony was perfect. Maggie Lu tossed the silk petals from her basket while Faith made attempts to pick them up and put them back. Tyler walked between them carrying the rings on a pillow Judy had made just for the occasion. Judy was escorted down the isle by her son and father. She kissed each of them tenderly as she stepped next to James. Alicia stood by her side as her witness and Marshall stood by his father as his. The little church was filled with family and friends. Molly and Tim were there from Texas with their infant son and Margaret was there with her fiancé Josh. Brad and Jen sat with Matthew and Jasmine while Faith Hope waved to them from her place at the altar. James' mother, father and siblings were all in their places along with Judy's family. Shirley and Terry were capturing the special moment with pictures and video and Cheryl and David helped quiet the grandchildren present. James' relatives all lived close by so they made up most of the attendance along with a few of the couples' close friends.

There was a song that Judy had heard one day on KPGY called *Bless the Broken Road,* by Rascal Flats. The lyrics told the story of meeting someone new after having previously loved and included the following verses:

I set out on a narrow way many years ago. Hoping I would find true love along the broken road. But I got lost a time or two; wiped my brow and kept pushing through. I couldn't see how every sign pointed straight to you.

Every long lost dream led me to where you are. Others who broke my heart, they were like northern stars; pointing me on my way into your loving arms. This much I know is true, that God blessed the broken road that led me straight to you.

I think about the years I spent just passing through. I'd like to have the time I lost and give it back to you. But you just smile and take my hand. You've been there you understand. It's all part of a grander plan that is coming true.

Every long lost dream led me to where you are. Others who broke my heart, they were like northern stars; pointing me on my way into your loving arms. This much I know is true, that God blessed the broken road that led me straight to you.

Now I'm just rolling home into my lover's arms. This much I know is true; that God blessed the broken road that led me straight...to you.

It was a love song that seemed to have been written just for Judy and James and their life together. That song became the theme for their wedding. Judy decorated the auditorium for the reception with stars. There were crystal star candle holders down the center of the tables. She even found a graphic with a road and falling star which was used for their invitation design. It represented the falling star she had wished on that first night they met. Marshall's wife, Tina sang that song beautifully for them as they lit their unity candle during the ceremony.

"I will never forget this moment," Judy thought as she gazed into those beautiful ocean eyes; facing the man soon to be her husband. It was time to repeat their vows to each other.

As James placed the tiny gold band on Judy's finger, he looked into Judy's eyes and repeated his vows. She placed his large ring on his finger and did the same. It was as if they were floating through the ceremony and they were all alone. Their focus was on each other, that precious moment would be locked in their minds for eternity. She heard nothing but his voice, saw no one but him and she could tell by the look in his eyes, it was the same experience for him. At the prompting of the priest, they kissed; sweetly and sincerely.

James embraced his new bride and whispered gently in her ear, "I love you, honey!" They stood their holding each other briefly as if to grasp the final seconds of their magical moment before turning to face their family and friends.

"I'd like to introduce to you, Mr. and Mrs. James Mac Donnell." The priest announced and everyone applauded as the organ played and the bride and groom walked briskly down the isle holding hands and smiling at family and friends.

"C'mon Jude! Toss the darn thing!" Jessica's voice rang out from the back of the hall where she stood with her husband Ted. They were the host couple for the reception. "They're all waiting!" Judy was suddenly brought back to the moment.

"Here it comes…ready or not!" Judy said as she flung the bouquet back over her head praying silently, "God please have it go to the one who'll be next…"

There were shrieks and laughter and the sound of people scrambling to the area where the coveted prize was headed. Judy turned to see who made the catch. The crowd burst into laughter

156

because Judy had over thrown the bouquet and it landed in the lap of the non-participating, unsuspecting Alicia…seated at a table across the room.

"Mom!" Alicia said as she stood with the bouquet in hand, I wasn't going to participate! I…I mean…I don't know…I don't even plan…I don't think…" she was at a loss for words.

Judy walked over to her daughter and held her close and whispered, "Sometimes we just don't know…or plan…or think. We just need to have faith and hope…remember?" Alicia had tears in her eyes, remembering the words of her sweet grandmother and hugged her bride-mother closely.

"Can I have this dance, Mrs. Mac Donnell?" James approached his new bride and gently took her small hand in his. Once again they were all alone in each other's eyes as the DJ from KPGY played *Bless the Broken Road*…and they swayed to the rhythm of the music, holding each other close.

"I love you, Mrs. Mac Donnell," James whispered to his new bride.

"I love you, too, Mr. Mac Donnell…forever." Judy leaned her head against his chest, thankful for this third chance at love and God's wonderful grace…remembering with joy her new beginning at Third & Grace.

Printed in the United States
102422LV00001BA/97/A